Charles P. Kirkland

A Letter to Peter Cooper

on Treatment to Be Extended to the Rebels Individually ...

Charles P. Kirkland

A Letter to Peter Cooper
on Treatment to Be Extended to the Rebels Individually ...

ISBN/EAN: 9783337252748

Printed in Europe, USA, Canada, Australia, Japan

Cover: Foto ©Raphael Reischuk / pixelio.de

More available books at **www.hansebooks.com**

TO

PETER COOPER,

ON

"THE TREATMENT TO BE EXTENDED TO THE REBELS INDIVIDUALLY,"

AND

"THE MODE OF RESTORING THE REBEL STATES TO THE UNION."

With an Appendix

CONTAINING A REPRINT OF A REVIEW OF JUDGE CURTIS' PAPER ON THE EMANCIPATION PROCLAMATION,

WITH A LETTER FROM PRESIDENT LINCOLN.

BY

CHARLES P. KIRKLAND.

NEW YORK:

ANSON D. F. RANDOLPH,

No. 770 BROADWAY.

1865.

A LETTER

TO

PETER COOPER,

ON

"THE TREATMENT TO BE EXTENDED TO THE REBELS INDIVIDUALLY,"

AND

"THE MODE OF RESTORING THE REBEL STATES TO THE UNION."

With an Appendix

CONTAINING A REPRINT OF A REVIEW OF JUDGE CURTIS' PAPER ON THE EMANCIPATION PROCLAMATION,

WITH A LETTER FROM PRESIDENT LINCOLN.

BY

CHARLES P. KIRKLAND.

NEW YORK:
ANSON D. F. RANDOLPH,
No. 770 BROADWAY.
1865.

MR. PETER COOPER:

In compliance with your request, I have written out, briefly, my views on two subjects of vital importance and absorbing interest, namely, "The Proper Treatment of the Rebels *individually*," and "The Mode of Restoration of the Rebel *States* to the Union." Believing these views to be correct, I publish them in the humble hope that they may receive the approbation of my fellow-citizens.

Your friend,

CHARLES P. KIRKLAND.

LETTER.

REVEREND thanks to God! the battle is fought and the victory won! After a contest of four years of unexampled proportions, in which hundreds of millions of treasure have been expended, and hundreds of thousands of lives have been sacrificed, the glorious end has come; reason, right, justice, liberty, humanity, have triumphed; the great truth is demonstrated that "man is capable of self-government;" the hearts of all lovers of free institutions, here and everywhere, are filled with rejoicing; the philanthropist witnesses with emotions of unspeakable delight the utter extinction of Slavery in this land, and, by necessary consequence, very speedily in every other; and in this death of slavery the American statesman sees the removal for ever of the great disturbing cause of his country's peace, the source of all the discord, heart-burnings and dangers of the Republic for the last half century. This gave life to the Rebellion, and retributively by the Rebellion it died!

The contest has in its progress and in its results exhibited, on the part of the defenders of the country, all the highest qualities of man: heroic courage, patient endurance, unshrinking resolution, persistent patriotism, unexampled military skill, noble generosity; while at the same time it has shown an extent of material power and resource, of which we ourselves had no adequate conception, and of which other nations were wholly ignorant. It is no vain boast to say that "the United States of America" *now* have an elevated, influential and distinguished place among the nations. The name of "American citizen" will *now* be an honored and respected name wherever it is known or heard. These great results have been obtained through enormous expenditures of money and of life; but who will say that the end is not worth the means? that the great cause of civilization, of free institutions, of civil and religious liberty, indeed, of Humanity, has not received a benefit equivalent to the costly price which has been paid? How joyous and blessed is this hour to those who, from the very inception of the Rebellion in December, 1860, by the adoption of the ordinance of secession in South Carolina, have with unwavering and cheerful confidence looked forward to the end now attained, and who with unclouded vision saw in a near future the salvation of their country! Rich now is the reward of their faith! Humbly and devoutly do the American people thank the Great Lord of all, that in His wisdom and goodness He has seen fit to grant such a termination to such a struggle, and thus to place the blessed institution of their fathers on a lasting foundation and to give us an assured faith that they can and will be transmitted in all their strength and beneficence to future generations. He gave to the men of the Revolution the wisdom to create this beautiful temple; to us of this day He has vouchsafed the successful performance of the task of defending and preserving it. Oh that the American people may manifest their earnest gratitude to Him for this great deliverance! not only by their words but by their works; by the more extended cultivation and practice of His precepts, the less engrossing devotion to matters of material and personal interest, and by a higher and purer love of country; such a love as will embrace the North, South, East and West in the bonds of a common and an affectionate brotherhood, will allay all sectional jealousies, and will carry out to its beautiful results the divine injunction, "On earth peace, good will toward men."

This mighty struggle having thus been brought to a practical close by the overthrow of the military power of the Rebellion, two questions of exceeding magnitude present themselves for immediate decision: First, "The treatment to be extended to *individual* rebels;" and, second, "The manner of restoration of the rebel *States* to the Union."

These questions I propose to consider.

I.

THE TREATMENT TO BE EXTENDED TO THE REBELS INDIVIDUALLY.

In the discussion of this subject passion and prejudice should be wholly discarded, for it concerns alike the highest earthly interests of many individuals and the present and future welfare of our country; and no one who justly appreciates its importance can speak or write upon it without a deep sense of responsibility. On its just decision will, in no small degree, depend the future " weal or woe " of the Republic.

To arrive at just conclusions, it is indispensable to consider the originating causes of the Rebellion ; the moral and legal offence involved in it ; the spirit in which it has been conducted by its authors, and by which it has been plainly. marked in its entire progress ; and after a dispassionate investigation of these matters, to consider what measures, as to the *individual* actors in this frightful drama, are required by justice, humanity and a due regard to the future peace and security of our country.

1. It cannot be doubted that the actual inauguration of the Rebellion is attributable to the unhallowed ambition of political leaders, born and nurtured under a system wholly antagonistic to our form of government, and whose keen perceptions exhibited to them, in colors of living light, the inevitable and not very remote melting away of the preponderating political power and influence so long exercised by their section and by themselves as its leaders ; this melting away being the necessary result of the difference in the practical working of the two systems of labor in the two great territorial divisions of the country. Had no such ambition existed in the breasts of prominent Southern men, the attempt to overthrow this Government *never would have been made*. Had *these* men been imbued with the spirit of the heroic and pure-minded Pettigru, the people of that region would at this moment have been in the full fruition of the same peace, happiness and security which, as citizens of " the United States of America," they enjoyed on the 21st day of December,* 1860, and which as such they had not for a solitary hour ceased to enjoy from the moment of the adoption of the Constitution in 1789 up to that (to them) fatally disastrous day. These leading conspirators had all ready a field wonderfully adapted to the consummation of their purpose of plunging their States into immediate rebellion. This field they had been for a long series of years assiduous in preparing for the harvest they were now about to reap. The people of those States were in general, at the period in question (viz., the inauguration of the Rebellion), deeply imbued with the following gross errors and delusions :

* The day of the passage of the ordinance of secession in South Carolina, and which was the practical birthday of the Rebellion.

(1.) They had come to believe that the whole population of the non-slaveholding States, with rare exceptions, were Abolitionists of the Phillips and Garrison school.

(2.) That the people of those States were mean and mercenary; that they were spiritless, cowardly and time-serving, ready to sacrifice every thing to their material interests; that, on the contrary the people of the rebel States were a brave, high-spirited, chivalric, generous race, superior in all things to those of the free States; that one Southern man was equal, in a military point of view, to three of the North; they regarded the name of "Yankee" as synonymous with all that was vile, dishonorable and contemptible; and the epithet "Yankee" they applied indiscriminately to all north of Mason and Dixon's line, alike to the German of Pennsylvania, the adopted citizen of Wisconsin, the New Englander of Vermont, and the Knickerbocker of New York. By necessary consequence, they believed that these "Yankees" would succumb at the first sight of the standard of rebellion and quietly yield to every demand. It is unnecessary to say how much this absurd but fatal delusion was fostered by the acts and the sayings of a large number of Northern men, justly denominated by John Randolph, in the bitterness of his withering satire, "dough-faces."

(3.) The lower class of their population, the "white trash," comprising an immense numerical majority, had been taught to believe, and did believe, that the sole object of the "Yankee" was to raise the negro to an equality with, if not to a superiority over, them.

(4.) The large proportion of that population, slaveholding and non-slaveholding, were therefore prepared to believe, and did believe, as they were assured in every possible form by the leading conspirators, that the election of Lincoln was the triumph of Abolitionism, that he was the favorite chief of that detested sect and the ready instrument of their will; and that *now* the only remedy was to cast off the yoke of the usurper and the tyrant.

(5.) The fatal heresy of the "right of secession" had for half a century been taught to those people as a fundamental truth, so that multitudes had embraced it as a primary article of their political creed. Its corollary was "allegiance to a State," so that the destructive error prevailed that a citizen of one of those States owed supreme fealty and allegiance to his *State* and none (when they came in conflict) to his *Country*.

How was it possible, it may be asked, that such errors and delusions could so thoroughly permeate such masses of men. The solution of the mystery is at hand; it is found in the benighted ignorance of those masses; and in those masses I include not merely the "white trash" just mentioned but many slaveholders. The great bulk of the latter live in seclusion on their plantations, seldom leaving their own State, and in numerous cases scarcely ever their own counties; with limited means of even common school education, as is shown by the national census; with a total suppression, as is universally known, of all liberty of speech and of the press on the subject of their "peculiar institution," seldom, if ever, in communion, either at home or abroad, with men of other parts of the world or other parts of their own country. This statement may seem exaggerated, but no man of ordinary observation, who has visited those States, will thus characterize it.*

* The reliable volumes ("Seaboard Slave States," "Texas Journey," and "A Journey in the Back Country,") of Frederick Law Olmstead, late General Secretary of the United States Sanitary Commission, fully confirm all these statements. A recent authentic publication as to the state of things in Texas (and it was the same in every rebel State) informs us that, "Perhaps there was never a people more bewitched, beguiled and befooled, than we were when we drifted into this Rebellion. We have been kept so to an amazing extent. Our editors, our preachers and stump-speakers, inflamed the people with falsehoods of rights violated, constitutions broken, laws disregarded, on the one hand, and easy victories on the other; and it is astonishing how easily the pretended secession was made and the war began. True, the people's ignorance made it an easy matter; but that does not excuse the persevering misrepresentations. Statements like this (by one since an officer of high rank) were common: 'I will give a good bond to drink all the blood shed in a war caused by secession.'"

Mr. James Brooks, now Member of Congress from New York, traveled extensively in the rebel States some years since, and published an account of his observations and experiences. In relating a conversation he had in South Carolina with one of the non-slaveholding class, who could read and was intelligent beyond his fellows, he says: "This conversation gave us a good idea of the feelings which have wrought up the mass of the people in South Carolina to such an exasperation. This man is by no means a specimen of the intelligent Nullifiers, but he is a good specimen of the backwoodsmen *who were to do the fighting*. The high mettled fellow had been first taught to 'damn the Yankees,' next, to cultivate an undue State pride; then, to believe his State was omnipotent, and her continuance in the Union all-important, and indispensably necessary to support the Government. He solemnly believed, and would have taken his oath, that South Carolina paid all the taxes of this vast Union. At a hundred million of dollars he set down her burden! A *foreign* nation was about to subdue him and his

There are doubtless exceptions to this general rule; men of culture, of high literary attainments and of varied accomplishments are found in those States; but the *mass* was without question in the condition I have stated. Ignorance is the genial soil in which to sow the seeds of error, delusion, prejudice; abundantly have those seeds been sown, and alike bountiful and baneful has been the harvest.

The wicked instigators of the Rebellion (while we cannot accord to them *sincerity* in the belief even of the doctrine of the inherent right of secession) *absolutely knew*, as no intelligent observer can doubt, the utter groundlessness of all the other errors, delusions and prejudices above-mentioned ; they were men, for the most part, of intelligence and education, and what is more, they had had full opportunity, by personal association with the people of the North, of knowing the falsity of the appeals they made to "fire the Southern heart." But those appeals were successful ; and. thus the originating cause of the Rebellion is found in the mad ambition of the conspirators, inciting to practical action a people laboring under an amount of error, delusion and prejudice unexampled in the world. The institution of " slavery" doubtless raised up this brood of conspirators and created a state of things favorable to the spread of these illusions : " Abolition" writers and orators furnished an abundant storehouse from which the conspirators drew the *falsehoods* on that subject, which they impressed *as truths* on their too willing listeners ; but further than just stated, neither " slavery" nor " abolition" was the immediate originating cause of the Rebellion.

2. It is difficult to find language to describe the moral and legal offence involved in the Rebellion. To say that it is a crime of greater magnitude than any recorded in history is but feebly to express its true character. It was a cold-blooded, deliberate attempt to overthrow the Government of the United States, to destroy the American nation, to inflict a deadly and fatal wound on the holy cause of free institutions and civil liberty here and everywhere, now

State, and his pride rose on the reflection, and he was ready to throw his life away in attacking a fortified castle on an open raft ! *Mr. Calhoun's well-instructed backwoodsmen of whom he boasted in Congress, are as ignorant of the extent, power, and complicated interests of this Government as are the Rocky Mountain Indians.*" He fully confirms all I have said as to the *non-slaveholding class*. He also equally confirms all my statements as to the ignorance, delusion and prejudice of that class of *slaveholders*, to whom I attribute those qualities.

and for ever ; it was *treason*, deep, damning and infamous. Its immediate consequences, to say nothing of mere material considerations, have been the destruction (including those on both sides) of at least half a million human lives, the grievous maiming, wounding or sickness of another half million, and the clothing in mourning of tens of thousands of households. For such a crime and for such consequences are those conspirators and their abettors legally responsible : they are responsible to God ; they are responsible to man.

3. It is an undoubted fact that the Rebellion, from its beginning to its end, has been conducted by the rebels in a spirit of savage barbarity. The deliberate plot to murder President Lincoln on his way to Washington in February, 1861 ; the massacre of the soldiers of the Massachusetts Sixth in the city of Baltimore on the 15th of April, and the assassination of Colonel Ellsworth at Alexandria on the 26th of May in the same year, were but the fitting precursors of the horrible slaughter at Fort Pillow ; the revolting and incredible cruelties inflicted on the soldiers of the Republic at all the prisons and prison-pens in the rebel States—Richmond, Danville, Salisbury, Columbia, Charleston, Andersonville,* indeed every place where any of them were

* At a public meeting at the Cooper Institute in April, 1865, the Rev. J. I. Greer, Chaplain of the One Hundred and Eighty-third Ohio, stated that, of the Union prisoners sent from Andersonville to Wilmington a few weeks since, not less than two hundred and eighty, in consequence of their barbarous treatment in that charnel-house, had suffered the excruciating torment *of the loss of their feet;* and upward of forty of those " footless" heroes are now in hospital at David's Island, in the harbor of New York !

At the risk of sickening the reader, but in stern regard to truth, the following extract from the Port Royal *South*, of May 6, is added :

" The steamer ' William P. Clyde' arrived here on the 3d, from Jacksonville, Fla., with nineteen Union officers and privates—part of a large number, supposed to be about 3,200, who are coming into Jacksonville every hour from the Andersonville prison-pen. The rebels brought them within a few miles of our lines and turned them loose. Nearly the whole number have already arrived at Jacksonville and are being provided for as well as possible by the Quartermaster's and Commissary's Departments of General Vodge's district. They are now receiving clothing and other articles necessary to making a decent appearance in a civilized community. Many of them are badly troubled with scurvy, chronic diarrhœa and other diseases. About thirty poor fellows were left at Andersonville, probably to die, as they were too sick to be removed. The following horrible account is furnished us by First Lieutenant M. G. Wilson, of the Ninety-ninth United States Colored Troops, who returned on the ' Clyde:' Statement of deaths among

confined in large or small numbers, whereby not less than fifty thousand as gallant and noble men as ever fought on any field were literally tortured to death or consigned to lingering and hopeless disease ; and the whole of this infernal work finally consummated by the deliberately-planned assassination of the head of the nation ! I do not dwell on those horrors—the bare mention of them is sufficient to cause a shudder through the civilized world. It is enough to say that these enormities could not have been perpetrated *in any other country professing the Christian faith ;* and here they can be accounted for only from the dehumanizing influence of slavery (as it has existed in the rebel States) on the white race, who had been under its operation for generations, and from the partial, if not the total, extinction of their moral sense by means of the crime of the Rebellion itself.

The state of feeling existing in the rebel States at the beginning of the Rebellion, as already stated, the error, delusion, prejudice, malignant hate, arrogant assumption of superiority, though not universal, were so prevalent that those deeds of matchless cruelty caused no shock to public sentiment there, but, on the

---

the Union prisoners confined at Andersonville, Ga., for the eleven months ending January 31, 1865.—February, 1864, 1 ; March, 282 : April, 576 ; May, 708 ; June, 1,201 ; July, 1,748 ; August, 2,991 ; September, 2,677 ;' October, 1,595 ; November, 494 ; December, 168 ; January, 1865, 199. Total, 12,640. The total number who have died at Andersonville since the establishment of that infernal pen exceeds 17,000."

The preceding are but an insignificant part of this horrible record. The authentic evidence on this subject, which has already been furnished to the public, would fill a volume of hundreds if not of thousands of pages.

Can it be believed that these awful barbarities had the deliberate sanction fo the rebel Congress ? Yet here is the proof. Among the documents found in Richmond after its capture, and now on file in the office of the Secretary of War at Washington, is the following resolution, introduced into that body, read the first and second time, and made the special order for the secret session of February 16, 1864 : "*Resolved, by the House of Representatives of the Confederate States, the Senate concurring,* That we do adhere to our opinion that the so-called Emancipation Proclamation of the President of the United States, and the enlistment of negro slaves in the several Federal armies now opposed to us, are not among the acts of legitimate warfare, but are properly classed among such acts as the right to *put to death prisoners of war without special cause,* the right *to use poisoned weapons and the right to assassinate,* and if persisted in, will justify this Government in the adoption of measures of retaliation."

And, after this, who will refuse credence to the statements of a correspondent of an influential paper of this city, writing from Washington on the 16th of May,

contrary, were received with favor. Multitudes of those people regarded the torture and murder of a "Yankee" (as in former times the Turks viewed the killing of a Christian) as a work well pleasing to God, and entitling him who performed it to heavenly rewards. We are informed, by official authority, that the assassination of the President was planned by rebels in Canada and approved in Richmond ;* but however this may be, no impartial observer of the events of the last five years can doubt that this enormous crime was the legitimate, if not the necessary, fruit and result of the teachings of the rebel leaders, and of the spirit in which they and their followers have conducted the war of the Rebellion ;† in other words, that the leaders are *morally* if not

1865 : "The question which has long been agitated as to who is responsible for the cruel treatment of our prisoners confined in Libby and other prisons in the South may now be considered as definitely settled, through no less a person that ex-rebel Senator Foote. It appears that Mr. Foote was a member of the Committee in the Senate to examine into the treatment of the prisoners and the reports of their harsh usage and starvation. His story, as told by his own relatives, show a deeper intention than has been generally supposed, and fastens upon Jeff. Davis and his Cabinet a crime both startling and appalling in its details. Mr. Foote, it is said, states that the investigations showed conclusive evidence that it was decided in Cabinet meeting to reduce the rations served out to the prisoners, that it should so weaken their constitutions in connection with the confinement that it would destroy them as soldiers, and make them when exchanged worthless. Senator Foote determined to report these facts to the Senate, but the balance of the Committee overruled him and suppressed the facts. My informant further states that it was on this point that the quarrel between Davis and Foote broke out afresh, which resulted in the latter leaving Richmond and seeking some sequestered spot where such horrid deeds were not committed. Here, then, is the evidence conclusive of Jeff. Davis and associates' guilt in the diabolical deed of starving our prisoners ; a deed which makes the most stoical person shudder to contemplate. Men who will coolly and deliberately plan a scheme like that will conspire to assassinate a President or any other person. It is a fitting sequel that authors of such deeds should end their career in a cowardly manner, dressed in petticoats. No wonder Jeff. Davis' cloven foot revealed who he was."

* President Johnson's proclamation of May 2d, 1865.

† The teachings and the spirit referred to are perfectly illustrated by the following extract from a recent paper (April 26), published at Shreveport, La. The editor, in commenting on the assassination of the President, says : " In one of his messages he said, with grim and terrible satisfaction, that under all circumstances our land would remain. Where the fierce Attila, calling himself ' the curse of God,' swept with his barbaric hordes, the historian records, as the marks of his terrible wrath, that ' he left only the sky and the earth remaining.' Attila, perhaps, joyed in the devastation. Abraham Lincoln, doubtless, did not. He may have felt pity, but no remorse ; and to fasten despotism upon a people free as himself, entitled to life and liberty and the pursuit of happiness, like himself,

legally responsible for this, the crowning crime of the Rebellion. Such, beyond question, is nearly the universal, as it is the just, opinion of our people.*

he would have stood unmoved and inflexible, and, with no eye turned to heaven, would have seen them swept from the earth, and only the land remaining, and felt himself a great Republican President, and one of the world's heroes. With all allowance for his amiable personal qualities, we yet know it to be true that Abraham Lincoln had as fell a purpose as ever existed in the bosom of despotism; that the Southern people should be bereft of their liberties, subjugated to a Government hateful to their inmost souls; and ruled for ever, not by their own free will, but by the bayonets and the votes of the more populous North. He was the instrument of the North to effect upon us and our children this destructive, ruinous object. Despotism has ever been insupportable to a free people; and, when practiced, even upon people whose spirits were broken and their pride degraded, its fit retribution has been the secret blow of the assassin, if not the open blow of the patriot. From 1787 to 1861 no guard had a President of the United States. He was the chosen officer of a free people, with no more concern for his personal security than that of the humblest individual in the land. If the reign of despotism is again to be re-inaugurated at this day, and over this people, then let despotism and whoever may be its minions beware the deserved fate of tyrants."

* From hundreds of proofs of the truth of this remark, I select the following: "At a meeting of the New York Board of Fire Insurance Companies held at the Insurance Rooms, No. 156 Broadway, on Monday, the following resolution was unanimously adopted and ordered to be published: '*Resolved*, That in the presence of this terrible crime, which is but a natural expression of that bitter malignity with which the Rebellion has been conducted from its inception, it would be a mockery to expect the nation, standing over the fresh grave of its noble, faithful and forgiving chief, to consent to strike hands with the bloody traitors whose instrument the assassin was, and permit them again to walk unscathed in the land which they have thus smitten anew.'"

"SAN FRANCISCO, *April* 17, 1865.—A large meeting of citizens was held at Platt's Hall, on Sunday, the Mayor presiding. A series of resolutions were passed, among which was the following, which amply expresses the general feeling on this coast: 'The great, capacious, manly heart of Abraham Lincoln was generous enough to have embraced all within the forgiveness of its loving nature. And in their madness they have killed him. Before his death the atmosphere was filled with generous emotions and kind sympathy. God have mercy on the souls of the rebel chiefs!' When this was read there was great excitement, and the people cheered over and over again."

"A large meeting of the cartmen of this city, was held Monday evening, in the Hall No. 95 Sixth Avenue, to take appropriate action on the death of the President, and make preparations to attend his obsequies. The following resolution was adopted: '*Resolved*, That the assassination of the President is but the culmination of the crime against the nation which commenced four years ago; that the same spirit which leveled the first gun against our flag in Charleston harbor, which initiated the murder in cold blood of the Union men of the South, which instigated the atrocities committed upon helpless prisoners, and which fired our city in the dead of night, inflamed the heart and guided the hand of the wretched

A subject of the deepest solicitude, and necessarily involved in the consideration of the question of the treatment of the rebels individually, is the *reconciliation* of the people of the two sections of the country. The people of the States which have not united in the Rebellion are, to a man, ready, cheerfully ready,

murderer, and justice demands that the malignant spirit of treason be utterly extinguished; that all the penalties provided by law be meted out to the instigators and perpetrators of the horrible crime known as the Rebellion, and that our land may know a just and abiding peace; that the human race may never again be cursed by a war so bloody and unnatural, for the sake of our posterity, and in the name of civilization we demand that justice be done upon the traitors who have desolated our country.'"

" At a special meeting of the Vestry of Trinity Church, held on Saturday, the 15th day of April, 1865, the following resolution was adopted: '*Resolved*, That while we regard the act by which our beloved country has thus been, through indescribable malice and fury, plunged into the deepest affliction, as one of those crimes of which no language can adequately paint the atrocity, of which the history of Europe has not for many centuries furnished a parallel, of which our own history has afforded thus far no example, and than which no history presents a more detestable and infamous act to the view, we cannot but hold it to have been dictated by the spirit, which, from the commencement of our national troubles, has sympathized with the enemies of the public peace, and aided and abetted the Rebellion now, as we trust, subdued; a spirit whose tendencies and essential character had previously been manifested in the July riots, in this city, in 1863; in the attempt to destroy the city by incendiarism in November last, and in the systematic outrages inflicted on our captured soldiers in the prisons of the South."

These show the concurrence in this view of all classes of our citizens.

And how can we doubt the correctness of this prevailing opinion, when we read in a leading rebel paper such articles as the following—in the *Chattanooga Rebel* (published at Selma) of the 20th of April, 1865: " William H. Seward, the cold-blooded and heartless political miscreant, who guided the infernal policy which plunged us into this bloody and desolating war, has been arrested by an angry God in the midst of his iniquities, and has paid the penalty of his crimes at the hands of an unknown assassin. Abe Lincoln, too, the political mountebank and professional joker, whom Nature intended for the ring of a circus, but whom a strange streak of popular delusion, elevated to the Presidency—he, also, has fallen. His career was as short as it was bloody and infamous. He has gone to answer before the bar of God, for the innocent blood which he has permitted to be shed, and his efforts to enslave a free people."

Let it not be said that this is only " a newspaper article;" conductors of public journals do not utter sentiments *revolting to their patrons.*

And when we add that at a large meeting at Shreveport, La., on the 26th of April, at which, among others, were present the rebel Generals E. Kirby Smith, Price, Buckner and Governor Reynolds, Colonel Flournoy of the rebel army appealed to the feelings of his auditory and received their hearty concurrence in his views. He concluded his address by a glowing panegyric on Booth the assassin, whom he " compared to Brutus the assassin of Cæsar, and predicted for him (Booth) a like and enduring fame !"—*Shreveport Sentinel*, April 27, 1865.

for this reconciliation. They are ready, with exemplary una-
nimity, to cast the veil of oblivion over the past; to pardon
the grievous wrongs they have suffered as a people and as individuals, and to welcome back to brotherhood the people of the
rebel States; but for their own sake, as well as for the sake of
those people, this receiving and welcoming back must be in such a
manner as to insure its *mutual* cordiality, and the *perpetuity* of
the blessings to flow from it to all. It is manifest from the statements already made of the state of feeling in the rebel States at
the commencement of the Rebellion, that no real reconciliation can
be effected so long as the errors, delusions and prejudices, mentioned as then existing there, continue. In the very first place,
the people of those States must at once and for ever part with the
absurdly (I may say ridiculously) false idea of their own "superiority," and the consequent inferiority of the rest of the nation.
It may well be believed that the delusion of their superior physical courage and "fighting capacity;" their idea that one man of
the South was, in this regard, equal to three of the North, has
been dispelled by the hard but inexorable "logic of facts." The
innumerable individual instances of the sublimest heroism, and the
steadiest courage in our soldiers; the skillful handling of large
Union armies in every one of their States; the numerous brilliant
victories which have given our officers and men a universality and
immortality of fame; and our final triumphant success will have
presented the truth in this particular in the clearest light to
the mind alike of the slave aristocrat and of the commonest of
the "white trash." They cannot but be satisfied by evidence
equally plain and irrefragable that they were laboring under
a similar delusion in their idea of the mean, mercenary,
selfish, craven character of our people, for they have seen
throughout every quarter of the North, even its remotest
hamlet, constant exhibitions of unselfish patriotism, of stern devotion to duty, of generous charity, indeed of every quality that
elevates and adorns humanity; they have seen life, fortune, domestic comfort, personal ease, love of kindred, every thing offered
in profusion on the altar of the country. Moreover, in our will-
ingness to receive them again into the common fold, they will see
a spirit of elevated magnanimity and of true Christian love, of
which the world has as yet furnished few if any examples. If

there be any of high or low degree in those States whose eyes are not opened by this overwhelming array of facts, such, beyond all doubt, are unfit to be "American citizens." But on every principle of human reasoning and of human action, it cannot be long before this great but indispensable revolution in the feelings and opinions of the mass of people of the rebel States will occur, and produce its beautiful and lasting fruits of peace, harmony and love.

In considering the subject of the restoration of harmony between the *people* of the two sections, it must ever be kept in mind that the leading conspirators and the arrogant slave aristocrats of the South, form but a very small minority of that people and that our business of conciliation is not with them chiefly, but mainly with the *millions of whites*, whom they have so long held in subordination, and the nearly equal number of blacks, whom they have so long held in slavery. The idea that that *South* which is to be reconciled and conciliated is the *slave aristocracy*, is an idea alike fallacious and injurious, and the sooner it is abandoned for ever, the better for the great cause in which we have, by the favor of Heaven, so signally triumphed. No ; it is not with that *handful* that we have to deal, but our business is with the *seven or eight millions* of other human beings dwelling on that soil. As to that numerically insignificant minority, we offer to them all, with comparatively few exceptions, the great privilege of returning "home," on the sole condition that, when they are readmitted to the house of their fathers, they will conduct as *brothers* of the household, and not as strangers, enemies, aliens or *masters ;* not as "superiors," but as equals.

Having thus concisely reviewed the originating cause of the Rebellion, the crime it involved, and the spirit in which the rebels have conducted it, we come now to speak of the treatment to be extended to rebels *individually.*

(1.) The very first idea that occurs here is the manifest distinction between different classes of those people, and I assert no more than I know to be the feeling of all in all parts of the Union, who have been steadfast in its support, that no terms or conditions are to be imposed, and no pains or penalties inflicted on the *mass* of the people of the South. They have grievously erred, but they have received an equally grievous punishment in the great suffering

2

they have endured in the unholy cause into which their wicked leaders seduced them. May Heaven forgive them as we do !

(2.) In determining this question, there are various classifications to be made of the comparatively small remainder of that people. " Treason " is conceded by all to be the very worst of crimes ; that its punishment should be in proportion necessarily follows. But it is the dictate alike of reason, justice and mercy, that a discrimination should be made in the punishment of the guilty, while we at the same time know that punishment to a proper extent is demanded by every consideration of humanity ; that it is required alike by God's law and man's, and that if we would, we could not as moral and responsible beings, avoid the performance of that duty, though we fully realize that in its performance we are bound by equally high and imperative considerations to temper justice with mercy ; to limit, as far as consistent with the public safety and with *true* mercy the number to be punished, and of that number to inflict the *extreme penalty* on as few as possible, and among the rest to graduate it according to their several circumstances.

(3.) Nor is this a matter of difficult practical solution. First, a small number of those men should without delay be indicted for the crime of treason. The humane, just and enlightened would, it would seem of necessity, include in this *class* the following :

(*a.*) The two surviving members of the Cabinet of Mr. Buchanan and the then Vice-President, all of whom, with unspeakable depravity, betrayed their country by using their official positions *to inaugurate the Rebellion ;* and with them should suffer that man, who, alone of his brethren of the Supreme Court of the United States, prostituted to the same unhallowed purpose the august office confided to him by his country.

(*b.*) The representative head, called the President, of the Rebel Confederacy, and all who have been members of his Cabinet.

(*c.*) Those members of the Senate and House of Representatives of the United States who, while in the exercise of their sacred trusts at the Capitol of the nation, deliberately, and with malice aforethought, committed the crime of treason in the face of the solemn and repeated warnings then and there given by their colleague who now (wonderful coincidence !) is invested with the power of making practically manifest the truth of what he then so impressively declared.

(*d.*) Each and every man who has by direct and responsible act participated in the murder, by torture in rebel prisons, of the soldiers of the Republic. The whole world stood aghast a few years since at the atrocities of the Sepoys of India; those were "tender mercies" compared with the cruelties just mentioned.

(*e.*) Each and every man who has by direct act participated in the murder of Union citizens in any rebel State.

(*f.*) Those who have acted the infamous part of rebel emissaries and representatives in Europe; * who by a continued system of flagitious falsehood have obtained there the material means of sustaining the Rebellion, and by which means alone it was sustained after the first eighteen months of its existence, and who have been ceaseless in their efforts to bring discredit, disgrace and ruin on their country. Thousands of the deluded victims of their frauds and deceptions in England and other parts of Europe would rejoice in common with us to know that such criminals had met the just reward of their treason and their fraud.

Probably many regard the above list as too limited ; possibly others may regard it as too extensive ; but let those latter consider that the aggregate number is in reality inconsiderable.

But humanity itself demands that men guilty of treason, *and such a treason*, every one of whom is *morally* guilty of the murder of all who have fallen in this war, and many of whom (as those mentioned under the third and fourth subdivisions) are guilty of actual murder, should at least be *placed in a position to receive* the severest punishment known to human law. Let no misplaced philanthropy, no unmanly sentimentality, no delusive idea of clemency be interposed between *such criminals* and their indict-

---

* The emissary Mason, in a letter dated April 27, 1865, published in England, and in which he attempts to defend the leaders of the Rebellion against the charge of complicity in the assassination of the President, dared to say : " As to the crime which has been committed, the people of the South will know, as will equally all well-balanced minds, that it is the necessary offspring of all these scenes of bloodshed and murder in every form of unbridled license, which have signalized the invasion of the South by Northern armies, unrebuked certainly, and therefore instigated, by their leaders, and those over them." If the combined crimes of treason and the blackest moral perjury are deserving of punishment, what should be the fate of this man ?

ment for treason. We are a civilized, a Christian, a humane people ; as such we now owe a stern duty to ourselves, our posterity, *our* country and the world. Let us with manly courage and dignity perform it !

There is no formal or technical difficulty in indicting each and every of those men for treason. Under the Constitution, treason consists in "levying war against the United States," or "adhering to their enemies, giving them aid and comfort." The rebels in organized association "levied war" against the United States ; they were thus legally and practically "their enemies ;" all mentioned in the preceding class were the participants in the actual "levying of war," or, what is tantamount, "adhered and gave aid and comfort" to those who were, and all were thus alike guilty of treason. It cannot be material *where* such "aid and comfort" were given ; wherever given by citizens of the United States, it renders them guilty of the crime. The prosecution of the indictment when found, and the carrying out the judgments in cases of conviction, rests with the Government, and in their hands will the people trustfully and cheerfully leave it. How many (if any) and which of the convicted criminals shall receive the extreme penalty must be decided by the President, with the aid of his official advisers ; that this decision will be governed by the highest considerations of duty, we unhesitatingly believe. From the necessity of the case, in many instances (such as the continued absence from the country of the party) the indictment, if found, could never be tried ; in other instances reasons might exist for not bringing on the trial ; in cases of actual trial and conviction the good of the country might be promoted by suspension or commutation of sentence, or even by pardon ; all these matters rest with the constituted authorities of the nation. But the voice of mercy, justice, national safety, cries aloud for the indictment for treason in each and all of the above cases. The moral influence of that proceeding would be alike beneficial and powerful, even if not one single step further were taken ; the indictment for a crime so awful would for ever hang *in terrorem* over the head of the guilty criminal ; would render him harmless for future injury to his country, and would keep him during life in a most healthful dread of a repetition of his crime ; it would operate, too, as a terrible and continuing warning to this generation and to many generations to come. It is possible that the President may consider that the ends of justice will be accomplished, and the safety of the country insured without bringing to the scaffold any of these great criminals; if, on the contrary, he sees fit to make this dreadful example of any one or more of them, the people will cheerfully respond, Amen! The vast majority of the humane, the just and the enlightened of our citizens, at this moment regard the infliction of the extreme penalty on one or more of the traitors as imperiously demanded by the plainest dictates of humanity and of duty. Time may alter their opinion.

It is to be remembered that in our country there is no power, executive, legislative or judicial, to *banish*, as can be done in England; and no power to deprive a citizen of his privileges as such, except after conviction for crime. It cannot be doubted that the " good of the country " requires that it should be for ever freed from the presence and the influence of the whole band of traitors above-mentioned, with perhaps an occasional exception. Objects so obnoxious and loathsome to the Republic cannot be tolerated here· Indictments for treason will *frighten away* those still among us, and will for ever *keep away* those now in foreign lands, and thus the practical benefits of lawful and effectual banishment will be attained.*

Second. Very few will doubt that the following persons (while unpardoned) should not be permitted to hold any office of trust, honor or profit under the Government of the United States :†

* An amusing, but by no means an alarming, spectacle is presented to us at this moment in the union of two most opposite extremes, namely, the pure, original Abolitionist of the one part, and the earnest sympathizer with the Rebellion and with the leading traitors of the other part, in urgent and clamorous opposition to any punishment of the traitors. It is quite manifest that no union of such discordant materials can be for good; and it is equally manifest that it must be wholly without influence on the Government or on the people.

†Congress has not the power to declare by law this incapacity, nor has the President that power, and no court can adjudge it till after a conviction for treason; but in this Government there is a power equally operative, namely, the " Voice of the People "—the *calm, deliberate, well-considered sentiment* of the American people always has had, has now, always should have, and always will have, the power of *law*. Under the influence of this sentiment, the appointing power would confer no office on *unpardoned* traitors; and if unfortunately any such should be sent from any State to either House of Congress, each House has the constitutional power to refuse admission to or to expel such person; and thus practically the same results follow, as if they were produced by statute or by a judicial judgment.

(*a.*) Every member of any State Convention, who voted in that convention for the *ordinance* of secession.*

(*b.*) All Governors of the rebel States during the Rebellion.

(*c.*) The rebel Vice-President, and all who have been members of the Senate or House of Representatives of the rebel Congress.

(*d.*) All who have been members of rebel State Legislatures.

(*e.*) All officers in the rebel army and navy above certain grades (and it would not be unreasonable to say, above the grade of colonel in the army and lieutenant in the navy), and all in army or navy of any grade, who have been officers of the United States Army or Navy.†

* Doubtless some of this class should be exempted from the general rule. The courageous Holden, of North Carolina, signed the ordinance of secession, under a physical and moral duress of unexampled severity; and he has since heroically exhibited his devotion to the Union. There may be others of other classes who, for special reasons, should have the privilege of a similar exemption; all such cases, we all know, will be calmly and kindly considered by the President.

† It is a grave question whether Robert E. Lee ought not to be indicted for treason. He violated his repeated oaths of allegiance and fidelity; he deserted the flag of his country; he carried with him, and doubtless communicated to the enemy, a vast fund of information derived from his official position as a member of the military family of Lieutenant General Scott; he falsified his assertion that he left his *country* to fight for his *State;* he has, by his personal and family influence, aided the Rebellion more effectually than any other single individual; he witnessed, day by day, for years, without sympathy, regret or protest, the murder by torture in the horrible prisons in Richmond of thousands of the gallant heroes of our Army, when a single word from him would have saved their lives and their indescribable sufferings; he is still an unrepentant impudent rebel, for, notwithstanding all the kindness and magnanimity shown him in the terms of his surrender, he had the hardihood immediately after to issue an order to his disbanded army, in which he says, " I congratulate you that your conduct has endeared you *to your countrymen.* I bid you farewell with increased admiration of your constancy and devotion to *your country:* you take with you the satisfaction that proceeds from the consciousness of *duty faithfully performed.*" Instantly on the issuing of this order, the man should have been arrested for *violation of his parole* in its spirit if not in its letter; for if the sentiments put forth in that document were adopted and acted on by those to whom it was addressed, they never could become in reality " Citizens of the Republic." The unhallowed fires of hatred to the Union would perpetually burn in their hearts, to burst out at any convenient time into treason. It is to be hoped that the Government will take the case of this individual into serious consideration, and decide whether he should not be subjected to a traitor's doom.

There are other rebel officers whom it would seem impossible to pardon: the General (Forrest) who perpetrated the savage massacre of Fort Pillow; the General (Picket) who ordered twenty-one prisoners of war, soldiers of the First North Carolina Loyal Regiment, to be placed in a row and shot; the wretch (Quantrell) who burned Lawrence, and murdered indiscriminately her men, women and children. These

(*f.*) Such private and influential individuals (not embraced in either of the above classes) as actively incited the Rebellion, and were conspicuous in inaugurating and sustaining it; a sample of these is the infamous Ruffin who boasted that *he put the match to the first gun fired at Fort Sumter.* On the same list stand those editors who, from the beginning to the very last moment, have contributed so much, so malignantly and with so much extravagance of falsehood to fan and keep alive the flame of rebellion. The injury done by them is incalculable. *

To say nothing of other official positions, what friend of the Union would not absolutely revolt at seeing either House of Congress desecrated, disgraced and endangered by the presence of

and all other similar monsters, are guilty of the double crime of treason and of actual murder. Their escape from the gallows would be a stigma on the humanity of the age.

* D. J. Baldwin, an honored citizen of Texas, and one of the few loyalists in that State, in a letter dated May 8, 1865, says: "Monstrous criminals as Davis and Lee are, the rebel editors have been their most efficient workers. Take a specimen or two of their efforts to keep up the spirit of their waning cause. It was solemnly asserted, and never denied by them, that Lee accepted four million dollars in gold as a ransom for the city of Philadelphia, in consideration of which he did not occupy and pillage the city. Another, that General Breckinridge occupied the President's House at Washington, and Jubal Early the Capitol, with their victorious troops; and the names of the soldiers were given who raised the rebel flag on the dome of the Capitol. These are two fair specimens of rebel military news. In civil and social matters they characterized and published biographies of our late President, as a bastard son of a mulatto woman by a drunken pauper; representing Northern society as disorganized; women corrupted, and men sunk in venality, lechery, and cowardice. And they are the men who have given the most efficient aid and comfort to the Rebellion. They did this at the bidding of Davis and his minions in rebellion and crime. They have given it hope and heart, which but for them and their acts it could not have had."

Down even to the last moment has the utterance of those monstrous and malignant falsehoods been continued by this class of men. The *Chattanooga Rebel*, of April 21, 1865, contains the following statement of the condition of things at Washington *after the assassination of the President:* "The last dispatches exhibit a most shocking and horrible state of society. The President and prime minister killed by assassins, and the new President and the Secretary of War murdered by a mob which has obtained and holds possession of the Capital of the nation. Other cities sacked, and a great popular revolution against the rulers impending. While their armies are devastating our land, their own down-trodden populace, infuriated by tyranny and driven to despair by want, burst the bonds of law, and a reign of terror and of ruin is established. That nation which prided itself upon its strength and prosperity, finds three different Presidents occupying its Executive Chair within the space of a single month, two of whom were murdered; discord and anarchy riding rampant and ruling the hour."

any one of that traitor band, until at least he had given the most unequivocal evidence of genuine repentance, and had received pardon from the President.

Confiscation of the property of the persons above-mentioned, in both the first and second classes, is eminently due to justice : (1.) justice to themselves ; (2.) justice to the country which, through their instrumentality, is subjected to a debt of three thousand millions of dollars, and to all its burdensome consequences.

Every individual embraced in this second class ought to be profoundly grateful if he is exempted from the punishment universally awarded by human laws to *Treason*. The President possesses the merciful prerogative of pardon ; his character and his solemn declarations alike show, that in suitable cases this power will be exercised with a pleasure proportioned to the pain, which the infliction of punishment causes to every generous heart.

It is earnestly hoped that none of the foregoing suggestions will be considered as indicating the slightest feeling of *revenge ;* that feeling is wholly unworthy the national dignity ; we have conquered, triumphantly conquered ; magnanimity, gentleness to the vanquished, so far as consistent with imperative duty, will be our crowning honor. These cases of disqualification and even of confiscation are within the modifying power of the Presidential prerogative, and that power will surely be exercised in every proper case.

Having thus briefly considered the treatment of the rebels *individually* in reference to actual punishment, it remains to speak of another branch of the subject not less important, namely, the course to be adopted in regard to the interior, domestic or social condition of that people ; in other words, in regard to "society" there. The term "*reconstruction of the States*" is loosely and inaccurately, though by no means infrequently used ; the term "reconstruction of society," in respect to those States, is a term of practical import and significance ; and this matter is of necessity involved in the general question of the treatment of the rebels as individuals. The truth of the proposition that "society" there must be "reconstructed" is self-evident. The annihilation of the cherished institution of slavery involves radical "social changes," the practical resumption by those people of their place in the

Union, after the events of the last five years, requires for the peace, comfort and harmony of us all, their abandonment of those errors, prejudices and delusions of which mention has already been made ; or at least the total cessation of all open manifestations of them. Without this, "reconciliation," sincere and true, cannot be hoped for. The habits of thought of that people, the manners, the false estimate of themselves and the consequent false estimate of the people of the non-slaveholding States, the tyranny of caste as to the non-slaveholding white class among themselves, all of which are the fruits of the existence there for so many generations of the institution of slavery, have created a "state of society" in those States, which has received its eternal death in the results of the Rebellion. "Old things have passed away and all things have become new," and to the "things" thus "become new," must the slave aristocrat and his sympathizers now conform themselves or go into voluntary or involuntary exile. When we speak of "Southern society" as heretofore existing, we of necessity mean only that composed of the slaveholder and his associates ; for, socially as well as politically, no other "society" has ever been known or recognized within the rebel States. The very first step in this "reconstruction" is the yielding up for ever by them of their arrogant fancy of "superiority," an idea acquiesced in, fostered, encouraged (in sadness be it said) by many, alas ! too many, of our people, those already mentioned as the John Randolph "dough-faces" of the North.* After the stubborn facts of the last few

---

* Notwithstanding the overwhelming triumph of the Union Army, this delusion of "superiority" and this contemptuous opinion of the "Yankee" are still rampant, as we know by authentic letters from every conquered city in that region—Savannah, Charleston, Richmond,—furnish abundant evidence. Rebel officers have dared to ostentatiously wear the "rebel gray" in the streets of those cities, and even in the Capital of the nation and in Northern cities. Witness, too, the supercilious impudence of Wade Hampton at the surrender of Johnston ; the brazen hardihood of Davis in his proclamation of the 5th of April from Danville, in which he says, that "no peace shall ever be made with the *infamous invaders* of our territory ;" the impertinence of the rebel officers confined as prisoners at Fortress Monroe, in adding at the end of their names, in a published letter on the assassination of the President, the odious letters "C. S. A."

A letter of April 26, 1865, from Washington, says : "Those who went hence to Dixie, four years ago, are returning by scores, generally in good health, shabbily dressed, *defiant*, and far from being hopeless in the ultimate success of their cause."

By a letter from Charleston of the 15th of April, we learn that : "The news of Lee's surrender arrived here by the 'Oceanus.' In the short space of a few

years, there is no longer a shadow of excuse for this arrogance. The facts have demonstrated the existence in profuse abundance among the heretofore despised and hated "Yankees" of the highest qualities of man, moral and physical courage, liberality, philanthropy, magnanimity, unsurpassed military skill, religious faith and reliance.

The change from "society" constituted as society in the Rebel States has been, to that in which no slave will be found; in which labor in its varied forms will be, as it should be, among civilized people, honorable and not degrading; in which thousands of immigrants from the non-slaveholding States and from foreign countries will form a part of the community; in which the heretofore despised multitudes of the subordinate white race will certainly, though gradually, be restored to manhood; and in which the "slave" is to be a "free" man: this change is indeed as total

hours the pardon of all the late rebels was discussed and considered as a fact. But it was received *as a right merely.* No gratitude was expressed toward the great General who forgave the great wickedness of this people."

A letter from Richmond, dated some days after its surrender, states that: "To-day there have been over a hundred rebel officers on the streets, most of them in full uniform, to say nothing of privates. Their hatred and bitterness has not abated one iota; they would do all the injury they could, and it is to be hoped that the order will soon be issued to register our enemies, and put an end to the parading of Confederate uniforms as a matter of glory and honor!"

Those instances might be indefinitely multiplied. Nor has Northern "toadyism" ceased. The colored troops were not permitted to participate in the first grand review at Richmond; a *colored* sentinel was removed from the house of General Lee's wife out of regard to her *feelings,* when her own husband had a few days before made the strongest possible appeal to the rebel Congress and people to send 300,000 *slaves into the rebel army* as soldiers; ministers of the gospel, belonging to the Christian Commission, paid an obsequious visit to the same General (an act since emphatically repudiated by the Commission by the dismissal of the offender); a Northern artist, about the same time, asked of the same General the privilege of taking the photographs of himself and the half dozen rebels that had formed his suite; some of our officers, on Lee's arrival at Richmond, as a paroled rebel prisoner, saluted him as they would have saluted Lieutenant-General Grant; the officer, who received the surrender of one of the large rebel armies, out of regard to the *feelings* of the commander of that army and of the rebels surrendering with him, prohibited the presence of representatives of the loyal press on the occasion; an officer, whose character is vouched for by an eminent editor of this city, writes from Richmond on the 12th of April, that: "An officer applied to one of the commanding Generals for quarters, and told him he would like to take a certain house. 'Whose is it?' 'It is that of an avowed secessionist of the blackest kind—the most infernal villain in the Confederacy.' 'Oh, certainly,' replied the General, 'you shall have it. If he's a rebel,

and radical as it will be enduring. To this change the old " society"
must yield ; the " society" hereafter will be in all senses " free"
and not " slave." It may be said, that the heretofore ruling class
will not be reconciled to the new order of things : then, as General Wool once happily said, " they may go, but they *must leave
to us their land.*" Again, all there must exhibit at least outward
respect to the Republic and its official representatives, civil and
military, who may be placed among them. The fatal heresy of
supreme allegiance to a State must be believed, if at all, in *silence ;*
no expression of contempt or hatred of the United States should
be tolerated.* *Above all, full and entire liberty of the press*, as
it now exists in the non-slaveholding States, must exist there.
And what a field is here for enlightened and patriotic editors !
How long, under the potent influence of a free press, would it be
before the bright light of truth would shed its beneficent radiance

of course you can have it for Government use. What is his name ?' ' Brigadier-
General Winder, of the rebel army.' ' No-o-o-o !' said the General ; ' No, you
can't have his house. Why, he was a classmate of mine at West Point !'. . . . . .
If you wish a favor from headquarters here, put on a gray uniform, and you can
get what you like. The officers of the late rebel army swagger about the streets,
sneering at the Union officers and are being coddled by the women of the town.
There appear to be more rebels in the city than Union men."

Many similar acts have dishonored us since our triumph over the Rebellion ;
and almost universally those acts are received not as evidences of generosity
and kindness, but as matters of *just due and of right.* Every such exhibition
confirms the Southern rebel in his illusion of " superiority," and postpones the
day that *must* ultimately come when that illusion will vanish for ever, and the
coming of which, as before remarked, is an indispensable prerequisite to *real*
reconciliation.

* General Burnside set the proper example on this subject. Soon after he
assumed command at Newbern, he issued the following wise and timely order :
" General Orders, No. 28—Headquarters Department of North Carolina, Newbern, April 28, 1862.—Whoever, after the issue of this order, shall, within the
limits to which the Union arms may extend in this Department, utter one word
against the Government of these United States will be at once arrested and
closely confined. It must be distinctly understood that treason, expressed or implied, will meet with a speedy punishment. The Military Governor of Newbern
is charged with the strict execution of this order within the bounds of his control.
     " By command of   Major-General BURNSIDE.
" LEWIS RICHMOND, Assistant Adjutant-General."

Had this example been faithfully followed in Washington, in Baltimore and
in every part of the rebel territory, as it became subjected to the power of the
Union, what numbers of valuable lives and what amount of pecuniary expenditure would have been saved to us !

over those people and dispel the moral and mental darkness in which, on *one* subject especially, they have never ceased to grope.

Again, in view of the great demoralization produced by the war throughout that region, and of the multitudes of soldiers of the late rebel army who will abound there, we may, for awhile, reasonably apprehend numerous acts of lawless violence,* insecurity to the persons and property of those who have not sympathized in the Rebellion ; interference in the free expression of loyal opinion ; words and acts of disloyalty to the Government, and other acts inconsistent with domestic quiet and security, and with the spread and growth of true Union sentiment. All this must be effectively and thoroughly repressed. It may be asserted that such a state of things cannot be brought about, but this assertion implies that *common sense*, as well as all regard to self-interest, have deserted that people ; and besides contradicts our uniform experience of the facility with which men accommodate themselves to *inevitable necessity*. This repression may be effected by civil power, or it may require military force. As to the latter, it is highly probable, nay, certain, that for a season its use will be indispensable in many parts of the rebel States, and to this end common prudence requires that a portion of our veteran army be retained there ; as much additional force as may be requisite for this purpose exists in abundance *on the spot :* a force which surely *the rebels* can have no scruple to our using, inasmuch as its use for military purposes was deliberately sanctioned and authorized and declared to be right by the rebel Congress at a period when men do not lie, namely, in its *expiring agonies*. This force, under the command of the humane, brave and experienced officers of our noble army

---

* The following extract shows what may not unreasonably be apprehended for the present in some portions of the rebel States. The *Alexandria Journal*, May 1, says : " Scouts from Fredericksburg report that that city and vicinity need the protection of the Government against rebel officers and soldiers, disbanded from Lee's army, who are now marauding upon the provisions and property of the inhabitants. Young men belonging to respectable families, who have been in the army, swear they will not work for a living, and devote themselves to plunder. Applications have been made to General Augur for a Provost-Marshal's establishment at Fredericksburg, to protect the citizens in their peaceful pursuits. The same thing will have to be done throughout Virginia. A letter from the borders of Loudon County, dated on Friday last, informs us that constant incursions are being made by these paroled rebel soldiers into Maryland, who drive off horses, cattle, etc., and tear down and destroy every American flag displayed in that neighborhood."

will be economical, safe and effective.* The dreadful state of
things brought about by the Rebellion and the deep-seated errors
and delusions from which it sprung, will, for a season, require
more or less of military government in all those States ; it will be
required till the most malignant of the slave aristocracy are disposed of by punishment or voluntary exile, and till truth and
reason have time to operate. But earnest is the hope, that the
necessity for the use of this force may be temporary ; it *must* be
so, unless the dogged obstinacy or the inveterate, unreasoning hate
of those, who have been, and would be again if they dared,
traitors, demand its long continuance.

It cannot, judging from the ordinary motives of human action
and the plainest principles of human reasoning, as has been already
stated, be long before most of those men, and certainly the vast
multitudes of the down-trodden whites of the South, will ap-
preciate the benignity, the blessedness, the priceless value of the
Constitution and the Union ; they will yet (and soon, we hope,)
love them as their Revolutionary fathers did. To effect these beneficent results, the people of the North, while extending cordially
the hand of brotherhood to the people of the South, must carefully
maintain their own self-respect and mark their sense of the great-
ness of the crime that has been committed, by refusing to *notorious,
blatant and unrepentant rebels* the courtesies of social life, by
sternly prohibiting among us any exhibition, by dress,† word or

---

* On this subject we have the emphatic testimony of the rebel commander-in-
chief. General Lee, in his letter of February 15, 1865, to the rebel Congress,
says : " The negroes under proper circumstances will, in my opinion, make efficient soldiers. Under good officers and good instruction, I do not see why they
should not become soldiers. They possess all the physical qualifications, and
their habits of obedience constitute a good foundation for discipline. They furnish a more promising material than many armies of which we read in history,
which owe their efficiency to discipline alone."

If they would make good soldiers in the cause of " slavery," it needs no reasoning to prove that they would make good soldiers in the cause of " freedom."

† This matter, it seems by the following order, is fully understood by General
Stoneman, and his example should immediately be followed everywhere :

"Headquarters District of East Tennessee, Knoxville, Tenn., May 6, 1865.—General Orders No. 31—Hereafter, any person found within the limits of this command
wearing or having about his person the badges, insignia, or uniform of an officer of
the late Confederate armies, will be considered as guilty of an act of hostility toward
the United States Government, and will subject himself to arrest and imprisonment.
By command of Major-General Stoneman. G. M. Bascom, Major and A. A. G.
—Official, G. M. Bascom, A. A. G."

act, of Southern arrogance and of rebel sympathy, and by ceasing for ever, in our treatment of the fossil remains of the slave aristocracy, from that, which, for want of more elegant expressions, is designated by the terms "toadyism" and "flunkeyism," and which has for half a century been too common among us.

We are not to overlook the vast aid, in this matter of the "reconstruction of society," which will be given by that small band of devoted men who have steadily adhered to the Union, nor by that multitude who have been *unwillingly* led or forced into the Rebellion ; nor, again, by that large number of owners of slaves who, though of the slaveholding class, did not belong to the insolent, overbearing, and arrogant "slave aristocracy," and could not be included in that almost demoniacal class, commonly known by the name of "fire eaters." This "reconstruction" may require time ; but if wisdom, prudence, *firmness*, kindness, are combined in the execution of the work, we may well believe that, in less than half the time it has required to crush the Rebellion, the task will have been so far performed as to give us the perfect assurance of its entire accomplishment within an additional period of no greater length.

Some of the slave aristocracy will prefer exile to a state of things in which the poor white is to be restored to a state of manhood, and the slave to freedom ; and they will depart without regret or sympathy. Many years must elapse before the immense material injury inflicted on those States by the madness of the Rebellion can be repaired, and some time perhaps before the true mode of adapting the emancipated slave to his new condition will be discovered and applied ; but when all this is done, and we cannot doubt it will be at no distant period, those States will enter on a new career of prosperity and of honor, which, while it invigorates and elevates them as *States*, will immensely add to the strength, power, and durability of the *Union*. We shall then be, in every sense, *social* as well as political, a *united* people.

In treating of the "reconstruction of society," I repeat, for it cannot be too often repeated, that what has constituted "society" there has embraced numerically but an insignificant minority of the people ; that many of the members of the old slave aristocracy will never consent to live under the new system, and will voluntarily expatriate themselves, leaving their places to be supplied by others ; that these latter together with those of the old "society" who are willing to conform to the "new," will thereafter form the "society ;" that, instead of the frightful bugbear of depopulation, presented to us in such vivid colors of horror by the rebel aristocracy and their sympathizers, the result will at the worst be the departure of a *few*, while the *millions* will be left, and the place of these few be supplied by men more worthy the privileges and the name of "American citizen." A careful estimate of the numbers embraced in all the classes, which have been mentioned in this paper, as being required by every dictate of justice and of true mercy to pay the penalty to a greater or less extent of their treason, will present but a *few hundreds* out of their *five millions* of white inhabitants. It is worse than idle then to predicate barbarity, cruelty, inhumanity, of the punishment those men may receive from a country whose life they deliberately and persistently sought to destroy, and hundreds of thousands of whose citizens have, *by their act*, been consigned to untimely graves.

II.

THE MODE OF RESTORATION OF THE REBEL STATES TO THE UNION.

It has already been remarked that the term "reconstruction," as applied to the rebel States, though often used, is used very inaccurately, not to say injuriously. It implies *ex vi termini*, the previous *destruction* of that which is to be *re*-constructed. In the case before us it implies that those States, *as States of the Union*, are destroyed ; that they do not now exist as such ; consequently, that the ordinances of secession were valid ; and again consequently, that a State has the *power* to withdraw from the Union. It admits the power and the *right* of secession.

This is an error as palpable as it is dangerous, and should not for a moment be sanctioned even by inference or implication. No. Those States, *as States*, have never for an hour in a *constitutional and legal sense* been *out* of the Union ; they have ever been and now are substantive and component parts of it as truly as Massachusetts or Ohio. Very much has been written on the subject of the *right* of a State to secede from the Union, so much indeed, that the intellectual argument may well be said to be exhausted. It may with equal truth be said that further argument is wholly useless, inasmuch as the question is for ever settled, and a judgment alike solemn, unappealable and irresistible has been pronounced by the only sovereign power—the people.

If the mighty war, through which we have just passed and in which we have so entirely and gloriously triumphed, has established any doctrine or principle whatever, it is " that no State has the right or power to, or by any possibility *can*, withdraw from the Union, except by an amendment to the Constitution permitting it." The fatal heresy on this subject prevailing so extensively in the rebel States was, as has been already mentioned, one of the instrumentalities by which the leading conspirators were enabled to inaugurate the Rebellion ; it was a direfully active agent in this fratricidal work : to impress on it the seal of everlasting condemnation and to sweep it, as an operative principle, for ever from existence, was one of the objects as it is one of the blessed results of the war.

This judgment of condemnation, obtained by more than four years of deadly conflict and at such an amazing expenditure of life and of treasure, stands, and will ever stand, a proud monument of the intelligent understanding by the American people of the true nature of their Union, of their earnest devotion to it, and of their determination that it shall be *perpetual*. Never again can this wicked delusion have any practical influence or perceptible existence in this country or in any part of it ; it has lived its day, it has performed its unhallowed work of attempting the national *death*, and has in the attempt met *its own ;* it now lies buried in a grave of infamy without the hope or possibility of resurrection. If, after all this, any man in America is found still to cling to that delusion, and to write or to speak in its advocacy, his bitterest enemy could wish him no worse punishment than he will receive in the pity, the contempt and disgust that will await him on every side.

In determining then the mode of *restoration* of those States the very starting point, the first step in the process, is the postulate, that, one and all, they have never ceased, since their admission into the Union, to be, and that they now are members of it, States within it.* With this rule as the guide, and with a faithful adherence to it, all difficulties in the way of restoration vanish.

It may be asked what is meant by "restoration," and what is the difference between that and "reconstruction." The meaning of the latter has already been stated; the necessity for the use of the former term arises from the fact that through the unconstitutional, illegal and void acts of citizens of those States, those States and the people thereof have for a period *practically* omitted to exercise their rights, enjoy their privileges and perform their duties in the Union; though *in the family*, they have been refractory, rebellious and disobedient members; their rebellion being at an end and they desiring to be again in the enjoyment of their wonted rights and privileges, and in the performance of their duties as members of the family (from which they have been for a season separated *in fact* but not *in law*), the question is how that "restoration" is to be effected. This brief "statement of the case" explains clearly the meaning of the term "restoration," and shows the propriety of its use.

1. A necessary consequence of the proposition above stated (viz., that no State has been, or is now, out of the Union) is, that all acts of any bodies of men in those States by whatever name called, conventions, legislatures, congress, designed or intended and performed for the purpose of withdrawing that State from the

---

* How well is this truth stated in a letter from General Sherman dated at Savannah, January 8, 1865, to a citizen of Georgia. He says: "Georgia is not out of the Union, and therefore the talk of 'reconstruction' appears to me inappropriate. Some of the people have been and still are in a state of revolt; and as long as they remain armed and organized, the United States must pursue them with armies, and deal with them according to military law. But as soon as they break up their armed organizations and return to their homes, I take it they will be dealt with by the civil courts. Some of the rebels in Georgia, in my judgment, deserve death, because they have committed murder, and other crimes, which are punished with death by all civilized governments on earth. You may rest assured that the Union will be preserved, cost what it may. And if you are sensible men you will conform to this order of things or else migrate to some other country. There is no other alternative open to the people of Georgia.

"My opinion is that no negotiations are necessary, nor commissioners, nor conventions, nor any thing of the kind. Whenever the people of Georgia quit rebelling against their Government then the State of Georgia will have resumed her functions in the Union.' It seems to me that it is time for the people of Georgia to act for themselves, and return, in time, to their duty to the Government of their fathers."

3

Union, and all acts consequent on or produced by such attempted withdrawal or designed to aid in its practical carrying out, are each and every of them *merely void :* * so as to all similar acts of any pretended executive or judicial authority, the creature of the Rebellion. This proposition would seem self-evident ; the thing

* This has been emphatically and solemnly declared in a recent Executive paper of President Johnson, in which he pronounces " that all acts and proceedings of the political, military and civil organizations which have been in a state of insurrection and rebellion within the State of Virginia against the authority and laws of the United States, and of which Jefferson Davis, John Letcher and William Smith were late the respective chiefs, are declared null and void.

"All persons who shall exercise, claim, pretend or attempt to exercise any political, military or civil power, authority, jurisdiction or right, by, through or under Jefferson Davis, late of the city of Richmond, and his confidants, or under John Letcher or William Smith, and their confidants, or under any pretended political, military or civil commission or authority issued by them or of them, since the 17th day of April, 1861, shall be deemed and taken as in rebellion against the United States, and shall be dealt with accordingly.

" The Secretaries of State, War, Treasury, Navy, and Interior, and Postmaster-General, are ordered to proceed to put in force all laws of the United States pertaining to their several departments, and the District Judge of said district to proceed to hold courts within said States, in accordance with the provisions of the acts of Congress. The Attorney-General will instruct the proper officers to libel and bring to judgment, confiscation and sale property subject to confiscation, and enforce the administration of justice within said State, in all matters civil and criminal within the cognizance of the Federal courts; to carry into effect the guaranty of the Federal Constitution of a republican form of State Government, and afford the advantage and security of domestic laws, as well as to complete the re-establishment of the authority of the laws of the United States, and the full and complete restoration of peace within the limits aforesaid. Francis H. Pierpont, Governor of the State of Virginia, will be aided by the Federal Government so far as may be necessary in the lawful measures which he may take for the extension and administration of the State Government throughout the geographical limits of said State."

The case is also very strongly and truly put by General Wilson in the following letter to the rebel Governor Brown : " Headquarters Cavalry Corps, M. D. M., Macon, Ga., May 9, 1865, 2.30 p. m. Sir—In pursuance of instructions received this day from Hon. E. M. Stanton, Secretary of War, I have the honor to inform you that your telegram of the 7th inst., forwarded by my sanction, has been laid before the President of the United States, and the following are his reply and orders :

" 1. That the collapse in the currency and the great destitution of provisions among the people of Georgia, mentioned in your telegram, have been caused by treason, insurrection and rebellion against the laws of the United States, incited and carried on for the last four years by you and your confederate rebels and traitors, who alone are responsible for all the waste, destitution and want now existing in that State.

" 2. What you call ' the result which the fortunes of war have imposed upon the

created must derive its vitality and power from its creator; and where the latter is wholly and absolutely baseless, is without a particle of the spirit of life, and whose death in a constitutional and legal sense was precisely contemporaneous with its very appearance, in such a case, the attempted or pretended creations from such an origin all partake of its character; all fall with it; all are equally inoperative, void and dead *ab origine*. Here the parent, the source of every thing subsequent, was the ordinance of secession; on this was based the *new* State, the new constitution, congress, legislatures, every thing; not a moment of real vital ex-

---

people of Georgia,' and all the loss and woe they have suffered, are charged upon you and your confederate rebels, who have usurped the authority of the State and assumed to act as its Governor and Legislature, made acts treasonable to the United States, and by means of that usurped authority provoked the war to extremity, until compelled by superior force to lay down their arms and accept the result which 'the fortunes of war' have imposed upon the people of Georgia, as the just penalty of the crimes of treason and rebellion.

"That the restoration of peace and order cannot be intrusted to rebels and traitors who destroyed the peace and trampled down the order that had existed more than half a century in Georgia, a great and prosperous State. The persons who incited the war and carried it on at so great a sacrifice to the people of Georgia, and of all the United States, will not be allowed to assemble, at the call of their accomplice, to act again as a Legislature of the State, and again usurp its authorities and franchises. Men whose crimes spilled so much blood of their fellow-citizens, and pressed so much woe upon the people, destroyed the finances, currency and credit of the State, and reduced the poor to destitution, will not be allowed to usurp legislative power that might be intended to set on foot fresh acts of treason and rebellion. In calling them together without permission of the President, you have perpetrated a fresh crime, that will be dealt with accordingly. I am further directed to inform you, that the President of the United States will, without delay, exert all the lawful powers of his office to relieve the people of Georgia from destitution, by delivering them from the bondage of military tyranny which avowed rebels and traitors have long imposed alike upon poor and rich.

"The President hopes that by restoring peace and order, giving security to life, liberty and property, by encouraging trade, arts, manufactures, and every species of industry, to recover the financial credit of the State, and develop its great resources, the people will again soon be able to rejoice under the Constitution and laws of the United States, and of their own State, in the prosperity and happiness they once had. To all good people who return to their allegiance, liberality will be exercised.

"If any person shall presume to answer or acknowledge the call mentioned in your telegram to the President, I am directed to cause his immediate arrest and imprisonment, and hold him subject to the orders of the War Department.

"I am, sir, very respectfully, your obedient servant,

"Joseph E. Brown, Milledgeville, Ga.   J . H. Wilson, Brevet Major-General."

istence have any of them had, because the ordinance was wholly and absolutely null and *void for the reasons already stated.*

It is of the last importance to adhere throughout to the proposition, that no rebel State has been, or is now, out of the Union, and to accept the *legitimate* practical results of that proposition, whatever they may be. Nor need any apprehension be entertained as to those practical results, if the views above stated, as to the "reconstruction of society," and the "treatment of the rebels individually," are adopted and truly carried out. Let this be done, (and, as has already been shown, *it can be done*) and not many months, surely not a long period will elapse before that region will be cleared of the *leading spirits* of the Rebellion by their punishment or flight, or if they remain, by their quiet and grateful submission to the Constitution and laws of their country ; within a period not longer, the prejudices, asperities and delusions of *others* will disappear before the resistless light of Truth, and the great bulk of the people will embrace with earnest joy the blessings of the mild and paternal Government of their country in exchange for the horrors of tyranny, despotism and war, which they have so bitterly experienced during the last four years. Then, whether under existing or new State constitutions and laws, that people will become, more emphatically than they have ever yet been, worthy citizens of the Republic and safe depositories of the power reposed in them by the fundamental principles of this Government.

But not till then will there be peace, quiet, real and true reconciliation and harmony, whatever course may be adopted by the executive or legislative authorities of the Union.

It may be asked what is to be the condition of those States and the inhabitants thereof till this state of things is reached. The answer is, that they must, *ex necessitate rei,* remain in their present anomalous condition—but it is to be remembered that the duration of this condition longer or shorter *depends entirely on themselves.* They can be relieved from it, if they so elect, immediately.* The

---

* The following order for the military re-districting of the State of Virginia shows the *modus operandi* during this interval: " *First.*—The sub-district of the Roanoke, Blackwater and Appomattox, as hereinafter designated, will constitute the District of the Nottaway, under command of Major-General George L. Hartsuff, headquarters at Petersburg. *Second.*—The counties of Accomac, Northampton, For-

constitution and laws of each rebel State, as they pre-existed the ordinance of secession, are at this moment the constitution and laws of that State. This may to some seem a startling, nay, an inadmissible proposition; but when examined it will be found strictly true and practically safe and beneficent. It must constantly be borne in mind, that those State constitutions and laws are by the very *fundamental* principles of our Union *subordinate to the Constitution of the United States and to all legislative and Executive acts conformable to the Constitution*. The Constitution

tress Monroe and the sub-district of the Peninsula, as hereinafter designated, will constitute the District of Fortress Monroe, under command of Brevet Major-General Nelson A. Miles, headquarters at Fortress Monroe. *Third.*—The counties of Princess Anne, Norfolk, Nansemond, Southampton and Isle of Wight, will constitute the District of Eastern Virginia, under command of Brigadier-General G. H. Gordon, headquarters at Norfolk. *Fourth.*—The counties of Nelson, Amherst, Bedford, Campbell, Appomattox, Pittsylvania, Henry, Patrick and Franklin will constitute the District of Lynchburg, under command of Brevet Brigadier-General J. Irwin Gregg. *Fifth.*—The county of Henrico will constitute a District, under command of Brigadier-General M. R. Patrick. *Sixth.*—The counties of Mathews, Gloucester, New Kent, King William, Charles City, York, Warwick, and Elizabeth City, excepting Fortress Monroe, will constitute the Sub-district of the Peninsula, under command of Brevet Brigadier-General B. C. Ludlow. *Seventh.*—The counties of Middlesex, King and Queen, Essex, Caroline, Spottsylvania and Orange, will constitute the Sub-district of the Rappahannock, under command of Colonel E. V. Sumner, First New York Mounted Rifles. *Eighth.*—The counties of Hanover, Louisa, Goochland, Fluvanna, Albemarle and Greene, will constitute the Sub-district of the South Anna, under command of Brevet Brigadier-General A. C. Vorris. *Ninth.*—The counties of Surrey, Sussex, Greenville, Brunswick, Dinwiddie and Prince George, will constitute the Sub-district of the Blackwater, under command of Brevet Brigadier-General McKibbin. *Tenth.*—The counties of Mecklenburg, Lunenburg, Nottoway, Prince Edward, Charlotte and Halifax, will constitute the Sub-district of the Roanoke, under command of Brevet Major-General Ferrero. *Eleventh.*—The counties of Chesterfield, Amelia, Powhatan, Cumberland and Buckingham, will constitute the Sub-district of the Appomattox, under command of Brevet Brigadier-General C. W. Smith. Commanders of districts and such of the sub-districts as are not included in any of the districts above described, will report direct to these headquarters, and will constitute separate brigades for the purpose of enabling the commanding officers to convene general courts-martial. The commanders of districts and sub-districts are made superintendents of Negro affairs within their respective limits." To the same import is the following extract from the *New Orleans Delta*, of May 25, 1865 : "General Sheridan has assumed command of the Military Division of the Southwest, embracing the country west of the Mississippi and south of the Arkansas Rivers. General Canby has divided the Department of the Gulf into the following four divisions—Louisiana, headquarters New Orleans; Mississippi, headquarters Jackson; Alabama, headquarters Montgomery; Florida, headquarters Tallahassee. The citizens of Louisiana appear much gratified by the programme of the new military authorities."

and those constitutional acts are the "supreme law of the land."
Consequently, taking for example the State of South Carolina, at
this very moment she is in a state of Union, with her constitution
and laws as they existed on the 20th of December, 1860, with
such modifications, changes, and variations as are created by any
acts of the Executive or legislative power of the United States
conformable to the Constitution of the United States *and now in
force.* Thus, the provisions of the constitution, laws and customs
of South Carolina as to slavery are wholly done away by the Emancipation Proclamations of September, 1862, and January, 1863, if
those proclamations were a *constitutional* exercise of power by
the President ; in which case *not a slave* now exists in that State.
It is not proposed here to discuss the constitutional and legal
validity of those magnificent State papers, nor whether they produced the effect desired and intended by the President. It is
well known that he considered them clearly within his constitutional power, and that in his view they instantaneously struck
the shackles from every slave in the rebel States.* Those proclamations are mentioned simply by way of illustration ; the
Confiscation Acts of Congress might be referred to for the same
purpose, but it is deemed unnecessary at this time.

It is sufficient to say that, if those *Executive and legislative* acts
are authorized by the Constitution, they are at this moment the
law in South Carolina. In our wonderful and beautiful though
complicated system, not fully understood even among ourselves,
and quite unintelligible to most foreigners, it is as vitally important to the people to preserve unimpaired *legitimate State* rights
as it is to protect and preserve inviolate the rights and powers of
the national Government. Occasionally a foreigner has perfectly

* The question of the *effect* of these proclamations is at this moment of great
practical importance, and will continue to be so till the Constitutional Amendment
as to slavery is adopted by twenty-seven States. That this most desirable event
will occur in the course of the next year can hardly be doubted ; but as it may be
longer delayed, it is not deemed out of place to add to this paper, by way of ap-
pendix, the writer's argument in favor of the constitutional validity of the proclamation of September, 1862. An additional reason for doing so is that that argument
received the cordial approbation of President Lincoln, and as every thing from his
pen since his martyrdom is an object of interest to his fellow citizens, a copy of an
autograph letter received from him is also given. That argument is reprinted
verbatim as read by President Lincoln, in order that it may be seen exactly of what
he spoke.

clear and just conceptions on this subject, and when he adds to that accurate knowledge of our political system an enthusiastic admiration and a heartfelt love of our institutions, his views are entitled to the highest respect and consideration, and indeed should have the weight of authority. Of this class is the eminent and excellent Du Gasparin. His words at this juncture cannot be too deeply pondered, nor his warnings too carefully listened to by the American citizen. In his great work, "America before Europe,"* he says: "The independence of the States must be protected with jealous care." "I counsel no measure that would not be strictly constitutional. I should have grossly contradicted myself if, after having advised Americans to preserve their institutions and retain them at the end of the war as they were at its beginning, I had urged them to violate them in their fundamental principle. The *liberty of the* STATES is no less important to be maintained than the *sovereignty of the nation.* A rebellion by the South *against the Constitution* should not be combated by a *similar rebellion* by the North. The two original features of the American organization should neither perish in the furnace of civil war. It will be glorious to see the United States come out of it with their *local* independence and their *national* unity alike unimpaired."

Whatever momentary inconveniences may be suffered from a rigid adherence to the fundamental doctrines (1.) that "no State can secede from the Union, except by an amendment of the Constitution," (2.) that the rights of the *States* as States must be preserved inviolate; whatever those inconveniences may be, a just regard to the preservation of the Union and of the Constitution requires, that those doctrines be steadily kept in view, and on no pretence, in any degree, or in any manner, departed from. The present condition of the rebel States is simply this: The people of those States were in rebellion against the Government, and sought to destroy the Union by the overthrow of the Constitution; while in this condition, the performance of their duties and the fulfillment of their obligations as members of the Union, were by their own act prevented, and in a constitutional sense, their State functions in that regard (that is as members of the Union)

* "America before Europe," pp. 362, 367, 368. His other work, "The Uprising of a Great People," contains similar warnings.

were in a condition of suspension. The Rebellion is now ended in the only mode in which it could be ended, namely, by the total destruction of its military power; and those States never having been in a constitutional and legal sense out of the Union, but their duties, obligations and privileges having been merely in a condition of practical suspense for a season, and that suspension being now terminated, they *ipso facto*, return to the fulfillment of those duties and obligations, and to the enjoyment of those privileges. Without inaccuracy of language and without the danger of the implication of erroneous ideas, " restoration " to the Union, in a practical sense, may well be predicated of their present condition. The results which follow from this view of the matter are simple, safe and intelligible.

Bear constantly in mind the fact, that the Constitution of the United States, and all constitutional acts of Congress and of the Executive *now in force*, are the *supreme law* in each of those States—and the further essential and indisputable fact, that there is now, and there need never cease to be, in each of those States abundant *national* military power to insure implicit obedience to that Constitution and those acts.* And where then is the difficulty in this mode of "restoration?" All the civil officers of the *nation* can safely perform their functions; her judicial tribunals can exercise their powers and carry into execution their decrees; taxes, external and internal, can be assessed and collected, and every *national* duty enforced. It has been demonstrated in a former part of this paper, that the requisite military power abundantly exists. Is it said that any State (by way of example again, South Carolina) will not perform its duty to itself by resuming its internal State functions, either under its existing or under a new constitution; will not elect a governor or legislature, nor appoint judicial and other civil officers, nor send members to either branch of the national Congress? This, should it be the

* General Thomas, in a letter of the 22d of May, 1865, to the Legislature of Tennessee, has well stated what will be done by him and by our Generals in every rebel State. He says: " I am prepared to assist the civil authorities in every part of the State, both by securing the officers from personal violence when in the execution of their office, in holding courts, etc., and assisting them to capture and bring to trial all persons who offer armed hostility to the State or national Government, and will so assist the civil authorities of the State as long as the national Government affords me the means of doing so."

fact, would be a truly anarchial state of things; and at least, would indicate on the part of the people of that State, an utter disregard of all that the people of other States deem essential to their comfort, safety and well being. Yet of what imaginable consequence would it be to the United States, so long as that State (South Carolina) pays its taxes to the General Government, interferes in no manner with the collection of the national duties on imports at its seaports, and offers no obstruction to the due and regular execution of the national laws through the national judicial tribunals; in other words, so long as the Constitution and laws of the United States are fully operative? It has already been shown that the nation has now, and never will cease to have, the full and effective means of enforcing obedience to the national Constitution and laws in any State that has been in rebellion; and if obedience is not rendered voluntarily it can and will be compelled. Again, if that State refuses or neglects to appoint Senators or elect Representatives to the national Congress, no harm is done to the *nation;* the State absurdly and injuriously to itself throws away its privileges, but in so doing it inflicts no wound, not the slightest, on the nation; the national Senate and House are convened and organized as usual, and pass laws operative and binding alike on the people of every State, that State which chooses to be unrepresented and that which has its full delegation in each House. Suppose that the State of New York, or of Illinois, in a fit of senseless passion, neglected or refused to be represented in Congress, the wheels of the national Government would not thereby be arrested or even clogged for a moment in their workings; those States would render a voluntary or a compulsory obedience to the laws of the nation, and the loss by their wayward conduct would be to them as States and not to the nation. The remarks, applied to South Carolina by way of illustration, of course, equally apply to every State that has been in rebellion; and it is thus seen that all that concerns the United States, *the nation,* is, *that obedience be rendered to her Constitution and laws,* and that if any State chooses to be in a domestic point of view, in a condition of anarchy, and sees fit to deprive itself of its rightful power and influence in the national councils, the detriment under our wise and beautifully devised system is confined to that State, is local and territorial, and in no degree, not even the least, extends to the *nation*, or in any manner affects its power or prosperity, or retards its resistless onward-progress. But will South Carolina, will any State thus stultify itself? Will she deprive herself of the countless blessings of a well-ordered State Government; introduce *domestic* anarchy and discord; cast away her right of representation in the Legislature of the country? Why should she? No motive can be imagined for a course so suicidal and of such unmixed absurdity and folly; and it may well be believed that the world will never be called on to witness a spectacle so miserable and so revolting.

It is manifest from the foregoing consideration that the great duty of the Government of the Union under existing circumstances is, first: To adopt sure and unfailing measures to obtain obedience in every State and in every section of every State to the *national* Constitution and laws; to permit no violations of duty and no departures from loyalty to the *Union* by any man or any set of men; to tolerate nowhere any thing calculated or intended to preserve or foster the infernal spirit that led to the Rebellion —but on the contrary to adopt and pursue practically all such measures as will *extirpate that spirit for ever*. As has already been suggested, to accomplish these necessary and indispensable ends military force may, for a season (longer or shorter, according to the *will of that people*), be absolutely requisite; and, as has also been stated, this great nation has now, and always can have that force to the utmost required extent.

A second and an equally solemn and imperative duty of the national Government, is to preserve inviolate the rights guaranteed to *the States* by the national Constitution. Among those rights, confessedly are: (1.) The right to have such constitution and such laws for their interior and domestic government as they see fit, subject only to the condition that the "form of government" shall, in the language of the national Constitution be "republican."

(2.) The right to prescribe the qualifications of electors, that is, who shall and who shall not possess the elective franchise. It is very clear that without an amendment of the national Constitution, the national Government cannot interfere in this matter. But practically speaking, that Government has, under the Constitution, the full power to protect *itself* against any improper or injurious exercise of that power by the people of a State, for, first, each House is " the judge " of the qualifications of its own members, and thus can refuse admission to all deemed unsuitable or unworthy ; and second, each House has the power of expulsion of members. Thus, if the Legislature or the electoral body in any State were so composed as to send to the Senate or the House of Representatives a man dangerous to the Union, he could be refused a seat or could be deprived of it, if admitted. This is a perfect practical safeguard so far *as the nation* is concerned.

It is very clear from the foregoing considerations, that there is no lawful or constitutional mode in which the question of " negro suffrage " can be controlled or decided by the national Government ; the sooner this fact is understood and appreciated, and acted on by all, the sooner will there be a real and effective pacification and harmony throughout the land. Some regard the extension of the elective franchise to the black equally with the white as vitally essential to the peace and well-being of the country. If this view is conceded to be correct, it is hoped that none entertaining it would desire to attain their ends at the cost of *a violation of the Constitution.* But if there are such, they form but an inconsiderable class of impracticable enthusiasts. The *people* resolve, and will take care, that the Constitution, the ark of our safety, be preserved wholly and absolutely from desecration. How then is this extension of suffrage, if admitted to be of the very highest importance, to be obtained ? There are but two modes. First : An amendment of the Constitution in the mode prescribed by itself. Second : A steady perseverance in the work of the " reconstruction of society " in those States, and the consequent extinction there of the " spirit of the Rebellion," and the substitution in its place of the views, feelings and dispositions suited to the " new " state of things.

That this latter result, required as it is by the plainest and most persuasive considerations, *can* and will be effected has, it is believed, already been shown in this paper ; and when effected, it is certain that this subject (of Negro suffrage) will receive the most mature and enlightened consideration, and will be disposed of in such manner as philanthropy, humanity and the best interests of civilization and of the country require. It is not a " whisper of fancy " nor a " phantom of hope " to believe and to assert, that

at an early period we shall witness such a " reconstruction of
society " in the rebel States as is portrayed in the preceding
pages; and, as is beyond doubt, *indispensable* to the present harmony and the future safety of the Republic. Let all who look
with timid apprehension or gloomy foreboding at the present
state and the immediate future of Southern society remember
these facts.

(1.) That the military force of the nation is, and will continue
to be, fully adequate in every portion of every rebel State to
preserve perfect peace and order ; to suppress all exhibitions, by
word or deed, of disloyalty to the country ; to insure entire safety
to the judicial tribunals of the Union in the performance of their
functions, and to secure perfect respect and implicit obedience to
their judgments ; to enable all civil, ministerial and other officers
of the Government to execute their duties, such as assessors and
collectors of internal taxes, census enumerators, commissioners of
confiscated estates, marshals, officers of the customs.

(2.) That there is and always has been a " leaven" of loyalty in
every rebel State, which, though not sufficient to " leaven the whole
lump," will materially aid now in all works requisite for social
" reconstruction" and political " restoration."

(3.) The horrors of the last four years of war and of a despotism tyrannical and severe beyond precedent, render the great bulk
of the people of that region not only willing but anxious to enjoy
once more the blessings of peace, security and liberty.

(4.) The most obtuse and the most prejudiced rebel mind cannot fail to see in the *facts* of these four years the most overwhelming evidence of his gross delusion in every important particular
as to the *character* of his brethren of the North.

(5.) Self-interest, that great motor in human action, most pal-
pably and most imperiously demands of those people a full and
honest acquiescence in the " new" state of things ; it demands of
them a course of conduct which will at the earliest moment re-
move from among them the last remaining soldier of the Republic,
and will place them as their fellow-citizens of the North are placed,
in the perfect fruition of all the privileges of this, " the best Government in the world."

(6.) Let us all duly estimate the transcendent influence of a *free press* and of *free speech*, with which that portion of the Republic is now, for the first time in its history, to be blessed, and by which it is to be instructed, elevated and refined.

(7.) Consider, too, the genuine brotherly feeling toward the people of the rebel States which pervades the universal North ; no one among us is actuated by a spirit of revenge ; no one calls for indiscriminate punishment, all desire and demand amnesty, except in a comparatively small number of cases, where the stern demands of justice and a due regard to the future safety of the Union require exemplary punishment and the necessity of which will be conceded alike by those people themselves, by us and by the civilized world. Who can estimate the kindly and emphatic influence on the people of the South of this generous, forgiving, fraternal feeling so universal at the North !

(8.) Commercial and business relations in all their diversified ramifications are fast being resumed between the two sections. What a bond of unity and concord is this ! and how powerfully will it contribute not to "restore" matters to *their old condition*, but to create an infinitely better and happier personal and social intercourse between them and us.

(9.) Beyond question, the rebel States will hereafter be freed from the noxious presence of many a "slave aristocrat," many " a fire-eater," many a disturber of the harmony of the country : this will, indeed, be a great boon, and few, very few will be found to shed a single tear over the voluntary or involuntary expatriation of such persons ; scarcely any " so poor as to do them reverence."

(10.) The large addition that will almost immediately be made to the population of each of those States by citizens from the non-slaveholding States and by emigrants from the various countries of Europe, will subserve a highly useful purpose in the great matter of the " reconstruction of society," and the consequent preparation of the citizens of those States to perform well their duties as citizens of a Republic, in which a political and social aristocracy, founded on Negro slavery, will no more be known for ever.

To a community *thus regenerated*, all questions affecting the public weal, the rights of the citizen, whether black or white, and especially the great right of suffrage, may safely be committed.

Let it not be said that this regeneration may be long deferred or may never occur, for while it is believed *certain* that neither of these assertions will be verified by results, there can be no mistake in saying that patriotism and an enlightened love of the Union plainly declare, that the falsification even of those predictions would be attained at too costly a price by any, even the smallest, *violation of the Constitution.*

APPENDIX.

President Lincoln's Letter.

EXECUTIVE MANSION, WASHINGTON, *Dec.* 7, 1862.

CHARLES P. KIRKLAND, ESQ., *New York:*

I have just received, and hastily read, your published letter to the Hon. BENJAMIN R. CURTIS; under the circumstances, I may not be the most competent judge, but it appears to me to be a paper of great ability, and for the country's sake, more than my own, I thank you for it.

Yours, very truly,

A. LINCOLN.

To THE HONORABLE BENJAMIN R. CURTIS, LATE ASSOCIATE
JUSTICE OF THE SUPREME COURT OF THE UNITED STATES.

I propose respectfully, but with perfect frankness, to review
your recently published pamphlet on the subject of the President's
"Emancipation Proclamation" of September 22d, 1862.

This would have been done at an earlier day, but it is only very
recently that I first saw the pamphlet.

It is to be regretted that, regarding—as you profess to do—
this proclamation and that of the 24th of the same month,
as fraught with peril to your countrymen, you did not treat them
separately. They differ radically and essentially in subject and in
intent. The one is limited in its application to the rebel States,
the other applies equally there and here. The one involves ultimate results and consequences of the most important and enduring
character; the other is, in its very nature, temporary. The one
gives rise to considerations of a kind wholly different from, and
irrelevant to, the other; yet your pamphlet so confuses them together, that it is quite difficult, if not impossible, to discover what,
in your view, is the distinguishing fatal error of each. Justice to
the subject, which you declare to be of such momentous import;
justice to the Head of this great nation, whose acts you arraign as
bordering on, if not actually amounting to, the *crime* of usurpation; justice to the elevated position you so recently occupied,
required that you should at least have pointed out separately,
distinctly, and in the most lucid manner, the grounds on which
you base a charge of such magnitude. Instead of that, we have
here (to use a legal term with which you are familiar) a complete
"hotch-potch." These different and distinct matters are thrown
indiscriminately together; and, in many instances, no ingenuity
can determine whether your argument, your illustrations, your
deprecatory expressions, apply to the one proclamation or to the
other. But at present I shall, so far as I can, ascertain from your
pamphlet the specific complaints you make as to the "emancipation proclamation," and, if I err in attributing to you allegations

as to this, which you intended solely for the other, my error will, I trust, find an apology in the mode you have adopted of treating the two subjects.

Before going further, I may be pardoned for imitating your example, and saying a word personal to myself. In some essential particulars, I stand in the same position you state yourself to occupy. I, like you, "am a member of no political party." "I withdrew," as you did, "some years ago, from all such connections." I have generally, however, exercised my privilege as one of the electoral body; and at the last presidential election I voted against the present incumbent, and at the last State senatorial election I voted for the Democratic candidate in my district.

I, like you, "have no occasion to listen to the exhortations now so frequent to divest myself of party ties, and act for my country." I, too, "have nothing but my country for which to act in public affairs," and with me, too, "it is solely because I have *that* yet remaining, and know not but it may be possible to say something to my countrymen, which may aid them to form right conclusions in these dark and dangerous times, that I now (through you) address them," and make the effort to aid them in "forming right conclusions" as to your views, and the subject of which you treat. Thus, my work, like yours, is purely "a work of love."

It may not be amiss to say, that there are, in fact, but two parties in our country; one that is for the country, the other that is against the country. To the former belong the vast majority of the Democratic party and the vast majority of the Republican party, and the few (alas! so few) Unionists of the South; to the latter belong the fanatical abolitionists in the Republican party, the rebel sympathizers in the Democratic party and the Rebels of the South. To the party of my country belong, I say, the great majority of both the Democratic and the Republican parties; in other words, the vast majority of the "People" of the United States—I say so, because I cannot be persuaded that that majority, by whatever party name the individuals composing it may be called, are insensible to the blessings of the form of government under which they live, unaware and ignorant of the indispensable importance of the preservation of the Union to their existence as a nation—forgetful, basely, ungratefully forgetful, of the heroic struggles and sacrifices

of their Revolutionary fathers—deaf and dead to the earnest paternal farewell advice and warnings of Washington, lost to all sense
of patriotism and of public virtue. And as to the millions from
other lands, who are now "of us and with us," who have sought
and found shelter and protection and happiness in our Temple of
Liberty, and who with such gallantry have recently fought the
battles of "The United States of America," and who individually
belong to the Democratic or the Republican parties, I cannot believe that these men, whether as individuals they may be called
Democrats or Republicans, will ever consent to the overthrow of
that Temple, or to the breaking up of those " *United* States." But
notwithstanding this perfect conviction of mine, it is nevertheless,
as you say, not out of place for you or for me, or for any others
who choose to undertake the task, to " say something that may aid
our countrymen to form right conclusions in these *dark* and dangerous " (as you call them) "times."

These words, " dark and dangerous," in the connection in which
you use them, lead me to say another preliminary word before
coming directly to your argument.

These words assure me, that you belong to that class of men
among us, not large in number, but sometimes influential in position, who, from natural temperament and disposition, or from
aversion to strife of all kinds, or from a want of *proper appreciation*
of the *real character* of this rebellion, (I think chiefly from the latter cause,) honestly labor under a fearful distrust or a gloomy foreboding as to the result of the impending contest for the preservation of our glorious government and of our blessed Union. *I do
not belong to that class of men.* I do not now believe, fear, nor
apprehend, and never for a moment have believed, feared or
apprehended that a crime, such as this rebellion, a crime against
the Almighty and against humanity, wholly without a parallel for
enormity in the world's history, and the iniquity of which can
scarcely be expressed in any language known to us, I do not, I say,
believe that such a crime will be permitted to be carried to a successful end, so long as " God sitteth on the throne judging the right,"
nor until Truth shall cease to prevail over error, reason to triumph
over delusion, and Right to overcome wrong.* On the contrary, I

* In speaking of the *crime* of this rebellion, the difference in a moral point of view
between the *leading conspirators* and the *body of the people* of the South engaged in it

look with a clear faith and a cheerful confidence to the termination of this rebellion at no remote period, and to such a termination as will show to an admiring and approving world that this government, confessedly the most beneficent, is at the same time the most firm and enduring to be found on earth.

To proceed to the examination of your argument:

The first observation I have to make is, that throughout your paper you treat the proclamation substantially as if it were a proclamation of *absolute* emancipation in the rebel States; that is, were it *such a proclamation*, your argument would be *in substance* the same it now is.

Again, in your copy of it, you entirely omit the clause in reference to *compensation;* and it will be found that a portion, and no immaterial portion, of your argument, is based on the non-exist. ence of the *conditional* and *compensatory* parts of the proclamation. It is very clear, that a proper regard to truth and fairness would have required a conspicuous place in your paper for these two distinguishing features.

With these omitted or practically concealed, you could by no possibility attain the object you profess, namely, " the aiding your countrymen in forming *right* conclusions."

A fatal error underlying your whole argument is, that in substance and effect you treat and argue this matter precisely as you would have done had there been no rebellion and *no war ;* had the country been at peace; had you prepared and published your views in November, 1859, (if a similar proclamation had been then issued.) You throw the veil of oblivion over the last two years; you ignore the events that have occurred during that period and the state of things existing in the country on the 22d of September, 1862.

Though you wholly disregard it in your *argument,* yet you forcibly describe the *status* of the country on the day of its date.

should carefully be kept in view. The *former* are to be *execrated,* the latter to be *pitied;* and while the practical effects of the wickedness of the one and of the delusions of the other, combined in action as they are, are the same, yet we are never to cease to draw the *moral distinction* just mentioned. Any one who desires to know the secret and real causes of the Rebellion, the motives and ends of the arch-conspirators who originated it, will be gratified and instructed by a perusal of the article entitled "Slavery and Nobility *vs.* Democracy," in the July number, 1862, of the *Continental Monthly.*

You say, " The war in which we are engaged is a *just and necessary* war. It *must* be prosecuted with the *whole force* of this government, till the *military power* of the South is broken and they *submit* themselves to their *duty* to obey and our *right* to have them obey the Constitution of the United States as the supreme law of the land." You thus affirm that, at the date of that proclamation, we were and *now* are engaged in a *war, a just and necessary war—* a war *that must be carried to a successful termination* by the exercise of the *whole force and power* of the government. You might justly have added, that it is a war infinitely worse, on the part of the rebels who caused it, than a war with any foreign nation could be, in its inception; in the mode of its conduct by the rebels; in the motives of its originators, and the ends sought to be accomplished by it. It was then by necessary consequence a war, in which all the means—and more than the means—we might legitimately resort to *in a foreign war* might and *ought* to be used and rendered available to the utmost practicable extent consistent with the rules of civilized warfare.

What, then, if we were at war with a foreign nation immediately on our borders, and that nation had within its bosom millions of slaves? Can any one, versed in the slightest degree in the principles of the law of nations and the laws of war, for a moment doubt our *right* to declare and proclaim freedom to those slaves, in case that nation did not discontinue that war within a prescribed period?

It may be asked what would be the utility, the *practicalness* of such a proclamation? I answer in your own words, " I do not propose to discuss the question whether this proclamation can have any *practical* effect on the *unhappy race* to whom it refers, nor what its *practical* consequences would be on them and on *the white population* of the United States." You discuss and I discuss simply the *constitutional right and power* of the President, *under existing facts,* to issue that proclamation.

We, in this discussion, are to assume that, in the contingency stated in it, it will go into actual operation as intended. Then we are to inquire what the practical effect of its thus going into actual operation would be, not on the black nor the white race, but *on the war* the rebels have declared and are carrying on. It requires but a very limited knowledge of facts to answer this inquiry. If any one fact is demonstrated with perfect clearness in this contest thus far, it is, that the slaves in the States in rebellion have furnished to those States means *indispensable* to them for carrying on and sustaining the contest on their part.* Without the agricultural and domestic labor of the slaves, tens of thousands of whites, who have been and now are in the rebel army, could not have been withdrawn from the cultivation of the ground, and the various other pursuits requisite to the supply, for that whole region, of the actual necessaries of life. Without the slaves, their numerous and extensive earthworks, fortifications, and the like, their immense transportation of military stores and munitions, a vast amount of labor in camps and on marches, (to say nothing of the actual service as *soldiers*, said in many instances to have

---

* Thousands of illustrations of the truth of this statement might be given. Take this one: On the second day of November, 1862, Gov. Brown, of Georgia, "Commander-in-Chief," issued this edict:

To the Planters of Georgia:

Since my late appeal to some of you, I am informed by Brig.-Gen. MERCER, commanding at Savannah, that but few hands have been tendered. When the impressments made by Gen. Mercer, some weeks since, were loudly complained of, it was generally said that, while the planters objected to the principle of impressments, they would promptly furnish all the labor needed, if an appeal were made to them. I am informed that Gen. Mercer now has ample authority to make impressments. If, then, a sufficient supply of labor is not tendered within ten days from this date, he will resort immediately to that means of procuring it with my full sanction, and I doubt not with the sanction of the General Assembly.

After you have been repeatedly notified of the absolute necessity for more labor to complete the fortifications adjudged by the military authorities in command to be indispensable to the defence of the key to the State, will you delay action till you are compelled to contribute means for the protection, not only of all your slaves, but of your homes, your firesides and your altars?

I will not believe that there was a want of sincerity in your professions of liberality and patriotism when many of you threatened resistance to impressment upon principle, and not because you were unwilling to aid the cause with your means.

I renew the call for negroes to complete the fortifications around Savannah, and trust that every planter in Georgia will respond by a prompt tender of one-fifth of all his working men.

As stated in my former appeal, the General in command will accept the number actually needed.

JOSEPH E. BROWN.

The Governor, it will be seen, calls for "one-fifth of all the working (slaves) men." The slave population in Georgia, in 1860, exceeded 462,000; it is not an exaggerated estimate, that one in six of that population is a "working man;" this one-sixth is more than 77,000, and one-fifth of that number is upwards of 15,000. The call is therefore for 15,000 "working men," and this too in a single State, and for a limited purpose. And yet we have not the *right to try* to render unavailable to the "enemy" this powerful force!

been rendered by slaves,) could by no possibility have been accomplished.

The intent and design of the proclamation, its actual effect, if it has its *intended* operation, is to forever deprive the "enemy" of this vital, absolutely essential, and, as I have just said, *indispensable*, means of carrying on *the war*. In reason, in common-sense, in national law, in the law of civilized war, what objection can exist to our using our power to attain an end so just, so lawful, and I may say so beneficent and so humane, as thus depriving our "enemy" of his means of warfare? I do not believe that you, on more mature reflection, will deny the truth of what I have just stated.

But you say, "grant that we have this power and this right, they cannot be exercised *by the President*," and for the exercise of this power, he is charged by you with "usurpation."

A few considerations will show the fallacy, the manifest unsoundness and error of your views and arguments on this point. I may, in the first place, remark that the very *title* of your pamphlet, "*Executive Power*," is a "delusion and a snare." The case does not give rise to the investigation of the President's "executive power." The word "executive" manifestly and from the whole context of the Constitution, has reference to the *civil* power of the President, to his various civil duties as the head of the nation, in "seeing that the laws are executed"—to his duties in time of *peace*, though of course the same "executive" duties still continue in time of war; but to them,' *in that event*, are superadded others, which, in no just or proper sense, can be termed "executive," but which pertain to him *in time of war* as " Commander-in-Chief." These latter duties are provided for by the letter and by the spirit of other provisions of the Constitution, by the very nature and necessity of the case, by the first law of nature and of nations, the *law of self-preservation*. What is the meaning and intent of the constitutional direction to the President, "that he shall *preserve, protect, and defend the Constitution*," unless in *time of war*, he can do so in his capacity of "Commander-in-Chief," unless in *time of war* he shall have the power to adopt and carry out *as to the enemy* such measures as the *laws of war* justify, and as he may deem necessary? Is the Constitution designed to *do away* these laws, and render them inapplicable to our nation—in other words, is the Constitution a *felo de se?* It cannot be denied, that in time of war, at least, the President, while in a civil sense the "exec-utive," is at the same time the military head of the nation—"the Commander-in-Chief"—and as such *his* "command" is necessarily coëxtensive with the country.

I cannot, on this point, quote anything more true and more ap-posite than a paragraph of your own. *"In time of war, without any special legislation, the* (our) *Commander-in-Chief is lawfully em-powered by the Constitution and laws of the United States to do what-ever is necessary and is sanctioned by the laws of war to accomplish the lawful objects of his command."*

This is, undoubtedly, the constitutional law of the land, and being so, it of necessity upsets and overturns all your objections to the proclamation in question. The "lawful object" of the Presi-dent at this moment is to preserve the Constitution by putting an end to this rebellion. In order to do this, it is necessary to deprive the rebels of their means of sustaining the rebellion—one of the most effective and available of those means, as just shown, is their slaves; the intent and object of the proclamation are to deprive them of those means. The so depriving them "is sanctioned by the laws of war," and, consequently, this act of the President is, within your own doctrine, perfectly legal and constitutional.

The same argument which you make against presidential power was made in Cross v. Harrison, 16 Howard, 164, in the Supreme Court of the United States, in a case occurring during, and arising out of, our war with Mexico, in the judgment in which case you, as one of the Justices of that Court, concurred. In that case the President, without any specific provision in the Constitution — without any law of Congress preëxisting or adopted for the occa-sion, created a civil government in California, established a war tariff, and (by his agents) collected duties. The Court held that these acts (to use their own language) "were rightful and con-stitutional, though Congress had passed no law on the subject;" that "those acts of the President were the exercise of a *belligerent right;* that they were according to the *law of arms* and right on the *general principles of war* and peace." Who will allege, that the acts of the President on that occasion were not, to say the least, as unauthorized by the Constitution and the law as his proclamation in the present case? And yet you did not dissent from the judg-ment of the Court, you did not speak of those acts as acts of

" Executive " power, for the term would have been there, as it is here, wholly inapplicable ; you did not then charge the President with usurpation. The whole case there was, as it is here, a case arising out of *belligerent* rights and duties, out of a *state of war;* and the President's acts were there, as here, not in contradiction to, and disparagement of, the Constitution, but consistent therewith on the great ground that the Constitution nowhere repeals, but, on the contrary, from the necessities of its own existence and preservation, recognizes the *laws of war* in a *state of war*. Similar authorities in abundance might be cited, but it would be a work of supercrogation.

It may not be amiss, however, to refer in this connection to the honored name of John Quincy Adams, on the *very point* now in question, namely, the constitutional right of the President to issue *this* proclamation.

No citizen of this land will deny to Mr. Adams as perfect an acquaintance with the spirit and nature of our institutions, as minute a knowledge of the provisions, expressed and implied, of the Constitution, and as ardent a desire to preserve them in their purity, as were ever possessed by any man living or dead. He was distinguished, too, for the most delicate moral sense, the purest integrity, and the deepest conscientiousness. I think no man who has taken an official oath ever felt a more earnest and constant desire on no occasion to violate it. Now, Mr. Adams, while a member of the House of Representatives, in a debate in the House, on an important subject, in April, 1842, after stating that slavery was abolished in Columbia, first by the Spanish *General* Murillo, and secondly by the American *General* Bolivar, by virtue of a *military command* given at *the head of the army*, and that its abolition continued to this day, declares that "in a state of *actual war* the *laws of war* take precedence over civil laws and municipal institutions. I lay this down as the law of nations. I say that the military authority takes for the time the place of all municipal institutions, slavery among the rest, and that under *that* state of things, so far from its being true that the States, where slavery exists, have the exclusive management of the subject, not only the President of the United States, but the (subordinate) commander of the army has *the power to order the emancipation of the slaves*." This is the " true saying " of a great constitutional lawyer, a pure patriot, a conscientious man—indeed, I doubt whether any man in this country, whose position entitles his opinions to any consideration, will be found to concur in your views. They are not adopted —indeed, they are repudiated by the most prominent leader of the Democratic party. Thus, Mr. John Van Buren (in a speech before the Democratic Union Association of the city of New-York, on the 10th of November instant) said: "I never said anything in reference to that proclamation except that it was a matter of questionable expediency. I have *never* deemed it *unconstitutional*. I have never even asserted that, as a *war measure*, it might not have been expedient." It would seem idle to add more in demonstration of the clear, unquestionable *power* of the President (I may say, of his solemn *duty*) "as commander-in-chief," in the exercise of a military power, "during a state of war," to issue the proclamation in question.

The ground of objection you most prominently put forth is, indeed, extraordinary, and, without offence, I trust I may say monstrous. It is no more nor less than this: "The persons who are the subjects of this proclamation are held to service by the *laws of the States* in which they reside, enacted by State authority." "This proclamation by an executive decree proposes to *repeal and annul valid State laws*, which regulate the domestic relations of their people," and this "as a punishment against the entire people of a State by reason of the criminal conduct of a *governing majority* of its people." Never was more error, gross, palpable, grievous, found in a single brief paragraph. Mark the existing state of things. These "States" are each and every of them in rebellion against their country and their Government; they are waging against it the most bloody and relentless war; they totally condemn and repudiate the Constitution of their country ; they deny that it has any, the least, authority over them; they are making almost superhuman efforts to overthrow and destroy it ; the people, as individuals, and the States in their corporate, municipal capacities, go hand in hand together in this awful work, and yet you claim for them the *protection* of that very Constitution ; you claim the inviolability of their *State* laws under *that Constitution*. You claim that those *laws* are "valid " and operative, and are to shield and protect, aid and assist them in their unhallowed attempt to destroy their country ! ! It is difficult to imagine under what hallucination you were laboring when you gave utterance to those sentiments. The bare statement of the case must carry to every sane mind, North and South, the instant refutation of your propositions. The very rebels themselves, to whom you offer the protection of the "Constitution," would, with wrathful indignation, spurn the offer.

You speak of the proclamation as a "threatened penalty"—as "a punishment to the entire people of a State .... by reason of the criminal conduct of a governing majority of the people."

I have already shown, satisfactorily I trust, that the act of the President partakes in no sense of the character of a "penalty" or "a punishment," but is simply the exercise of his constitutional power, in a time of war, to devise and adopt and carry out against the enemy such measures as he may judge to be for the good of his country; for the defeat of that enemy, and for the successful and speedy ending of "the war." You draw a distinction, unheard of, I imagine, till announced by you, a distinction between the "people of a State," and the "governing majority" of that people; a distinction, too, which is to operate, *in a time of war, against* the party with whom that "State" is at war ! ! I venture to say, that no writer on the law of nations, no judicial tribunal, no intelligent man, has up to this hour believed or stated that, in the case of foreign war above supposed, the "governing majority" was not to all legal and all practical purposes, "the State." Were the United States at war with any foreign power—a war sanctioned by the "governing majority," (as our war of 1812,) but a war which you and others (a minority) wholly disapproved; and that foreign power adopted some war measure which would operate on "the entire people" of the United States, could you and your associates of the minority, on any principle of law, military or civil, of justice, of reason, or of mercy, claim exemption from the effects of that measure ? The case supposed is precisely the case as it now exists between the "United States of America" on the one hand, and the "Rebel States and people" on the other.

Again, you state as a serious, if not conclusive objection to the proclamation, that "it is on the slaves of loyal persons or of those who from their *tender years*, or other disability, cannot be either disloyal or otherwise, that the proclamation is to operate."

Have your countrymen at this hour, to learn for the first time that the "sun shines alike on the just and on the unjust," that storms and whirlwind overwhelm at the same time the righteous and the wicked, and that the calamities of war, from the very necessity of the case, fall indiscriminately on the innocent and the guilty, the strong and the helpless, on those of mature and those of "tender years"? But as to this last objection, itlacks one material quality, namely, foundation in fact. That part of the proclamation which you have so strangely, as observed above, omitted, provides for the case of the very persons for whom your sympathies are excited. It pledges to them compensation. I say "pledges," for it declares "that the Executive will in due time recommend that all persons who have remained loyal (of course including in its spirit those who from tender years, or otherwise, were incapable of being disloyal) shall be *compensated* for all losses by acts of the United States, including *the loss of slaves.*" No future Congress of the United States will be so lost to all sense of honor and obligation as not to pass, and no future President so degraded as not to approve, a bill redeeming this solemn and sacred "pledge" of the Head of the nation.

Again, you advert in no part of your argument to the vital fact that this proclamation is not absolute and unconditional, but that it depends even for its existence *practically* on the acts and will of the rebels themselves. If they so elect, *it is never to go into operation,* and they have abundant time to make that election, namely, from the 22d of September, 1862, to the 1st of January, 1863. But your argument, *in all its essential particulars,* would have been just the same as you now address it to your fellow-citizens, if this proclamation had been absolute, had declared universal emancipation, to go into effect on the day of its date, and (as already remarked) had not provided compensation to the loyal, and had been issued in a time of profound peace.

You profess, in your argument, simply to examine "the nature and extent, and the asserted source of the power by which it is claimed that the issuing of this proclamation was authorized;" and it was "for the purpose of saying something to your countrymen to aid them in forming *right conclusions,*" that you 'reluctantly addressed them." The policy, the expediency, the utility, the practical effects, *per se,* of the proclamation, you say, you do not

" propose to discuss," yet you *intimate*, that by means of this proclamation, if executed, "scenes of bloodshed and worse than bloodshed are to be passed through," and you express, in no unequivocal manner, a doubt " as to the lawfulness, in any Christian or civilized land, of the use of such means (that is, this proclamation) to attain any end." You intimate, too, that "a servile war is to be invoked to help twenty millions of the white race to assert the rightful authority of the Constitution and laws of their country." All these direful forebodings are put forth in half a dozen lines, certainly not to " aid your fellow-citizens in forming right conclusions," but through their sympathies and their fears to induce the concurrence of their reason in your views as to the *power* to do the act in question. These "givings out" of yours require a passing notice.

In the first place, where is your authority for the allegations as to " scenes of bloodshed and a servile war ?" I am not an abolitionist, nor a believer in the *social and political* equality of the black and white races, (though I have an opinion on the subject of the effect of the *institution* of slavery on the white man and white woman, who have been nurtured under its influence, and on the question of the compatibility of the institution with a republican form of government.) I am even called by some a pro-slavery man. Yet I see no " scenes of bloodshed," no " servile war," in the event of the practical carrying out of this proclamation. This, however, is a mere matter of speculation and opinion, and while I freely concede your right to entertain your own, I claim my right to entertain mine. Our means of forming our opinions are the same; we both have the same lights, and the result alone can show which of us is right.

But, in the next place, assuming the consequences to be *just such* as you imagine, who is responsible for those consequences ? They cannot come, as you will admit, if the rebels *return to their allegiance ;* if they cease their unhallowed efforts to overthrow their government ; if they become dutiful citizens. If they do not, it is not your fault nor mine, nor that of our fellow-citizens, nor of the President, nor of the government of the United States—it is solely, wholly, unquestionably *their own.*

Again, you look with evident heartfelt horror at the events which you thus contemplate. Have you no horror, no tears of sympathy, no "bowels of compassion," when you reflect on the multitudes, the thousands of valuable loyal lives lost, homes grief-stricken, parents rendered childless, and children rendered orphans ; the desolation and misery of whole neighborhoods, to say nothing of the enormous material destruction caused to citizens of the loyal States in this war—a war on our part, as you say, "so just and necessary," and on the part of the rebels so wicked, so wanton, so utterly causeless, and so wholly unjustifiable? Though no man of humanity could look with other than deep distress on the "scenes of bloodshed," and the "servile war," you imagine, (should they become realities,) surely it cannot be believed, that the amount of distress and suffering, that would thus ensue, would equal — it surely cannot surpass — the distress and suffering that have already been endured by the loyal citizens of this republic in consequence of this rebellion.

You doubt the "lawfulness," in this Christian and civilized land, of the use of such means (as this proclamation) to attain *any* end. And has it come to this, that a distinguished citizen of the republic doubts whether a proclamation emancipating the slaves in those States which shall be in rebellion on the first of January next, may not be "used as the means" "to attain the end" (granting that it may *thereby* be attained) of ending this war of rebellion, and thus of saving our Constitution, our government, our Union, and of still preserving for ourselves and for coming generations, here and elsewhere, the only real Temple of civil and religious liberty in which men can worship on earth? You speak of "lawfulness" in this connection rather in a *moral* than in any other sense; the right and power in *a legal and constitutional sense*, to issue this proclamation has already been demonstrated.

In a document intended, "after study and reflection," "to aid the citizens of this republic to form a right conclusion" on matters of surpassing magnitude and solemnity — matters imperilling their very liberties, as you state — a religious, scrupulous regard to truth in every material respect, was of course, to be expected ; and departure from truth may consist as well in omission and suppression as in direct assertion. I have already mentioned that you have wholly omitted, in the statement of the proclamation, the compensatory part, and that you omit to bring forward, except merely incidentally, another most material part of it, namely, its conditional. *alternative* character.

Whether your statement as to the "social condition of nine millions of men," has reference to both white and black, or to the white only, it is difficult to determine from the context; if it has reference to the white, you commit a very serious error; for the whole white population of the rebel States, (to which alone the proclamation and your argument relate,) according to the last census, (1860,) does not exceed four and one half millions.

In quoting the opinion of the lamented Judge Woodbury, you omit to state that it was a *dissenting* opinion, concurred in by no other Judge, founded essentially, if not solely, on the fact assumed by him, that at the time in question in that case, "a state of war" *did not* exist in Rhode Island, where the matter arose. In so grave a paper prepared, as you assert, so deliberately, put forth under an imperative and resistless impulse of patriotic apprehension that the liberties of the country were in imminent peril, (not from the rebellion but from the acts of the President, designed to crush the rebellion,) in such a paper, I say, it would seem that we ought not to be terrified by "portentous clouds," "gigantic shadows," the phrase "usurpation of power," often repeated, the "loss of his head by Charles I.," "seven hundred years of struggles against arbitrary power," and many other similar appeals, *by modes of expression*, to anything but that *calm reason*, which enables us to "form right conclusions in dark and dangerous times." Much less in *such* a grave document from such a source, should important stress be laid on the expression, of an unnamed and irresponsible editor of a newspaper, "that nobody pretends that this act is constitutional, and nobody cares whether it is or not." That this editor was at least a very inferior constitutional lawyer, is very clear, and that this text from his paper should have furnished a peg on which to hang an alarming commentary on the "lawlessness" of the times, is at least extraordinary, and that lawlessness, too, *not* the lawlessness of *rebels* nor of *rebel sympathizers*.

You ask, in view of the President's proclamation: "Who can imagine what is to come out of this great and desperate struggle? The military power of eleven of these States being destroyed, what then? What is to be their condition? What is to be our condition?"

Your questions admit of a ready answer. *The United States of America* are to come out of the struggle, a great, a united, a powerful, a free people, purified by the fires of adversity, and taught by their tremendous calamities the lessons of moderation and humility. The *people of the rebel States*, who choose to remain in them, are to come out of the struggle as citizens of States forming a part, as heretofore, *of the United States*, and with them, and as parts of them, they are in future to enjoy the blessings of a well-regulated liberty, they having in the mean time been taught a lesson of infinitely greater severity than that by which their brethren of the loyal States have been instructed. Whatever they have necessarily and legitimately lost in material things, by reason of *the war* they have waged, is, of course, lost to them forever; if their slave property is thus lost, *it is lost*, and that is all that can be said as to that. Then "their condition" and "our condition" is to be *in substance* just what it was before the rebellion, and what it would have continued to be but for the rebellion, with this only difference, that they and we will have learned the priceless value of the Union, and for generations to come treason and rebellion will not raise their horrid heads.

Perhaps you may call this the dream of an enthusiast. Rely on it, I speak only the words of "truth and soberness;" and if you are spared for a brief period, you will be rejoiced, I trust, to witness their full realization. *Rejoiced*, I say, because from your pamphlet, you would have your countrymen infer, and I am bound to presume, that nothing but your intense love of your and their country and your agitating apprehensions that the "principles of liberty" are grievously to suffer, (not from *the rebellion*, but from the acts of *the President*,) has induced you to address them.

You say the "cry of disloyalty" has been raised against any one who should question these executive acts. I know not whether that epithet has been applied to you; if it has been, I am bound to believe that the imputation was without cause, and that you are a faithful, loyal citizen of the Republic. But the greatest and the best are liable to err, and I may be permitted to say, that, however honestly and sincerely you entertain the sentiments you express, you have selected an inopportune moment for their expression; and that at this particular period of our country's history, your "studies and reflections," your time and your efforts, would, to say the least, have been more benignly and gracefully employed in presenting to your countrymen a lifelike picture of the *real* character of this rebellion, and in impressing on them with stirring and glowing eloquence the momentous duty it devolved on them. You could, with perfect verity, have told them, that this war, inaugurated by the rebel States, was wholly and absolutely *without cause :* in proof of that assertion, you could have stated three facts, so undeniable that the hardiest rebel, not bereft of reason, would not dispute them.

First.—That on the 1st day of November, 1860, no people on the globe were in the more perfect enjoyment of civil and religious liberty, of social, personal, and domestic security ; of more entire protection in the possession and use of all their property, of *every kind ;* and of more material prosperity, than the people of the eleven rebel States.

Second.—That for all these blessings, as great as were ever vouchsafed by God to man, those people were indebted entirely to that Constitution and that Union which their rebellion was undertaken to destroy.

Third.—That from the day of the organization of the Government under that Constitution, in the year 1789, down to the day when this rebellion began its infamous and unhallowed work, there never had been, on the part of that Government, a single act of hostility, nor even of unkindness, toward these States or their people.

You should then have pointed out to your "countrymen," in language more persuasive and emphatic than I can use, their solemn and imperative duty as patriots, as Christians, and as men, in this hour of their country's suffering and peril ; and you should have told them that if these times are, as you say, "dark and dangerous," this darkness and this danger have been caused by the wicked acts of these rebellious men. In such an address to your countrymen, your dedication would have been not merely "To all persons who have sworn to support the Constitution of the United States, and to all citizens who value the principles of civil liberty which that Constitution embodies, and for the preservation of which it is our only security," but also, "to all persons who abhor treason and rebellion against that Constitution, and to all who prize the inestimable blessings of our hallowed Union, and to all who hold dear the farewell words of the Father of his country."

I had intended, in this letter, to comment on that part of your pamphlet which relates to the President's proclamation of the 24th of September, 1862, but this paper is already sufficiently extended. It would, I think, be easy to show that the dreadful dangers you apprehend are, in truth, to use your own terms, "portentous clouds" and "gigantic shadows" of your own creation. At any rate you may rest assured, if you and I and all others of our fellow-citizens, outside of the rebel States, shall make honest, earnest, determined efforts for the putting an effective end to this rebellion, (and that such will be the case I, loving my country and knowing the *unspeakable value of the stake*, have no right nor reason to doubt,) those efforts will be crowned with speedy and triumphant success, peace and harmony will be restored to the republic, the "principles of civil liberty" will not have suffered, and the bugbears of "usurpation," "arbitrary power," and other similar chimeras, which excited imaginations and gloomy tempers have evoked, will disappear forever.

Had you been an unknown and obscure citizen, any notice of your pamphlet would have been supererogatory; but because of the influence calculated to be exerted by anything coming from the pen of one who had but recently been the incumbent of the highest office in the gift of the Government, and who is now in the exalted walks of social and professional life, I have deemed it my duty to present these views of your argument, and thus "possibly to aid my countrymen" in "forming right conclusions" as to its merits and the merits of the subject of which it treats.

I hear that others have published answers to your paper. Not having seen any of them, I know not but that I may have merely repeated their views; if so, no harm is done; if I have presented any that are new, "possibly" some good may result.

New-York, Nov. 28th, 1862.

CHARLES P. KIRKLAND.